FINDING FOREVER

FINDING FOREVER

•

Liz Thompson

AVALON BOOKS
NEW YORK

PRINTED IN THE UNITED STATES OF AMERICA
ON ACID-FREE PAPER
BY HADDON CRAFTSMEN, BLOOMSBURG, PENNSYLVANIA

To my children, for filling my life with joy;
To my critique partner, Mary Schramski, for her
insight and friendship;
and
To Erin Cartwright and all the talented folks at Avalon Books
for making this book a reality.

Chapter One

Prince Charming had a black eye. Well, actually it was more than a black eye—almost half of nineteen-year-old Kyle Martin's face was swollen and gleamed black, blue, and faintly purple. A row of stitches zig-zagged across his left cheek toward his ear.

"Kyle, are you all right? What happened?" Blair Collins headed across the wooden stage in the high school auditorium to stand next to her co-star. Kyle was playing Prince Charming in the charity production of *Cinderella*. At the moment, it looked like he was in desperate need of a fairy godmother himself, which wasn't surprising. The young man was a walking magnet for trouble.

"It was great," Kyle said. From the way he spoke

1

out of the side of his mouth, he was obviously in pain. "I was playing left field, and that ball just came sailing right to me."

"That catch was a thing of beauty." Bob Julian, AKA "the King," looked at Blair. "The only reason Kyle caught the ball was because it hit him in the face, then plopped right into his glove."

Blair turned toward Kyle, who was beaming like he'd intended the play to work that way. "That must have hurt."

"Nothing I couldn't handle," Kyle said with a shrug.

"Well, isn't this just terrific. Kyle looks like a train hit him," Leigh Donnelly, the woman playing Cinderella, observed as she joined the group. "Now what are we going to do? Do you think makeup can cover that mess?"

Blair rubbed her throbbing right temple. This problem with Kyle was just one more in a long string of difficulties she'd encountered since she'd volunteered to direct the charity production of *Cinderella*. Up until now, Leigh had caused most of the ruckus. As the richest woman in the small town of Raynes, Texas, Leigh was used to getting what she wanted.

And she'd wanted Blair as the director, although why was anyone's guess. Blair had about as much in common with Leigh as a minnow with a shark. But since Leigh was the main lifeblood of Blair's accounting business, she'd done what most people in Raynes did when confronted by Leigh—she'd agreed to help. Her only consolation was that the production was for a good cause: all of the money raised would buy new toys for the children's ward at the local hospital. And for that, Blair would put up with the nonsense.

With a sigh, Blair surveyed the damage to Kyle's face. Makeup would never completely hide the defect. It was too large, too dark. Too black.

"Yeow. Check out the walking wounded," Theresa Anton said with a giggle. As one of the evil stepsisters, Theresa seemed to enjoy taunting Kyle almost as much as she enjoyed ribbing Leigh. "So much for your poster-boy looks, precious. We'll never be able to use you in the play now."

Kyle shot her as much of a sneer as his face would allow. "Ha, ha, Theresa. And even though I'd like to hang around to watch you fall flat on your face on opening night, I can't. I've decided to take off for New York. A friend thinks he can get a scout for a minor league team to take a look at me. Opportunity is kicking down my door."

Stunned, Blair stared at Kyle. "New York? Can't you wait until after the play?" she asked. This wasn't the first problem she'd had with Kyle in the two weeks they'd been rehearsing. Still, he was a warm body, and with just three days left until opening night, she couldn't be choosy. "Please, the children need us."

"No can do. Sorry. But it's been kicks." Kyle gave Blair a mock salute. "See ya."

As he walked toward the exit at the back of the high school auditorium, Theresa said, "Exit Prince Charming."

Most of the cast laughed, but not Blair. This was a full-fledged, stop-the-presses disaster, and the last thing she felt like doing was laughing. Still, she could handle this. She'd handled worse.

Trying to think over the chatter of the cast, Blair sat on a small folding chair on the side of the stage and considered her options. There must be some place she could find a new Prince Charming. Granted, she'd already been through two. First her brother, Eric, had volunteered to play the part, but he'd been in a nasty car accident and was laid up in the hospital. Thankfully, he was going to eventually be all right. But not soon enough to help.

Finding Kyle hadn't been easy. Not a lot of young men wanted to dress up as Prince Charming. Especially when Leigh Donnelly was playing Cinderella. The golden-haired beauty had a tough reputation and was going through husbands like tissues. She'd just split with number three despite the fact she wasn't much older than Blair's own twenty-nine.

"Good riddance to bad rubbish," Leigh said, smoothing her hands down the sides of her short designer skirt. "I never cared for him. He was too young to play Prince Charming. Plus, he was always rude to me."

Blair bit her tongue. After all, Kyle's desertion wasn't Leigh's fault.

"Well, we have to find someone else. Anyone have an idea for a replacement?" Blair asked the cast, hoping to solve the problem quickly.

"Maybe one of the high school boys would do it," Theresa said. "We must know *someone* who's got a kid who can be coerced."

Leigh planted her hands on her slim hips. "No way am I acting with some teenager."

"Kyle was only nineteen," Blair pointed out.

"Which was way too young. Don't you dare bring in another kid. I'll look like I'm a million years old standing next to him. Plus, I'm not kissing anyone under the age of eighteen."

"Roger might do it," Marci Gia, the evil stepmother, offered. "Although he'd have to use sick days to get the time off from work."

Leigh snorted in a very unladylike manner. "Marci, your husband looks no more like Prince Charming than I do."

"Hey, Roger's very attractive," Marci maintained.

"For a fossil," Bob said.

Marci moved toward him. "Like you can talk. Roger's only two months older than you are. You're just mad he made the varsity football team and you didn't."

Blair bit back a smile. She loved living in this small town, partly because of this quirk. Since most of the residents had spent their entire lives in Raynes, the people had a past together. They knew almost everything about each other, and they stuck together during tough times. Even though she was new in town, Blair already felt a connection to the other residents. She loved being part of the community.

Knowing the older woman meant well, Blair smiled at Marci. "Thank you for the offer, but it wouldn't be fair to ask Roger to use his sick days." Scanning the rest of the small group, she asked hopefully, "Any other ideas?"

A mumble went through the crowd. Several people shook their heads.

"Keep your hopes up." Theresa patted Blair's shoulder. "Maybe the perfect Prince Charming will just waltz right in."

Blair opened her mouth to answer when the aged wooden door in the back opened with a loud groan. Everyone stopped and watched as a tall, ruggedly built man with deep black hair entered. Even from a distance, Blair could tell he was handsome. In the sudden silence of the auditorium, she watched him walk down the center aisle. He had on well-worn jeans and a black T-shirt.

When he reached the stage, he flashed a lopsided grin at the group, and Blair felt as if her heart dropped to her toes. His eyes were as blue as Paul Newman's. The kind that made your pulse race and your palms sweat. *Yeow*, as Theresa would say.

"Anyone know where I can find Blair Collins?" the man asked.

"Guess you're not going to have to kiss frogs after all," Theresa muttered at Blair's side.

Talk about luck. Blair half suspected she had her own fairy godmother sitting on her shoulder. *Maybe, just maybe, things were going to work out after all.*

This was one weird town. Josh Anderson let his smile fade as he studied the small group on the stage. They stood looking at him like he'd dropped from the sky. He'd always known living in a small town made you a little screwy after a while, but this was ridiculous.

"I'm looking for Blair Collins," he repeated slowly.

A young woman moved forward. She had shoulder-length brown hair and wore gray slacks and a dark pink top. When she got closer, he saw that she had pale hazel eyes. He should have known that the one he found pretty would be Eric's sister.

"I'm Blair Collins," she said, her soft voice doing odd things to his equilibrium.

"Hi. I'm Josh Anderson." He glanced at the crowd,

starting to feel a little self-conscious. Why were they all staring at him? He resisted the impulse to make certain his fly was zipped. "I was over at the hospital, and Eric asked me to stop by and give you a lift after you finish." He shot another look at the group. "Didn't Eric tell you I was coming to visit?"

Blair shook her head. "No. But I'm not surprised. He sometimes forgets to mention things to me." She frowned, a tiny wrinkle appearing on her forehead. "Josh Anderson? You're his buddy from the Army, right?"

"Yeah." He glanced at his watch. "Eric thought you might be done soon, but if you're not, I'll just wait outside."

"Ask him," the red haired woman standing next to Blair whispered in a not-so-quiet voice.

Blair didn't acknowledge the woman's words. Instead, she smiled at him. *Wow, she really was very pretty.*

"I'm almost done," she said. "But we've run into a problem, so I may need a few more minutes."

"Ask him," the woman hissed again.

"Not right now," Blair muttered to the redhead without taking her gaze off Josh's face.

"I'll ask him." A tall blonde stepped forward. She was slim and beautiful but had cold eyes.

Instinctively, Josh took a step back. "Ask me what?"

"Nothing." Blair turned away from him and faced the group.

Whatever look she gave was enough to quell them—at least for the moment. In his book, it looked like now was a good time to escape.

"I'll be outside," he said and headed toward the exit. He knew they were all watching him. He could feel the skin on the back of his neck crawling. How many times had he felt that same sensation growing up? A hundred? Maybe more. Massey Falls, Oklahoma, was just like this town. Everyone watching everyone else. Wanting to know your business. Thinking they had the right to tell you how to live your life.

He shoved open the worn auditorium door and crossed the lobby at a clip, old feelings catching up with him. He wouldn't think about the past now. Not tonight. He was tired and hungry and countless miles away from Massey Falls. This uncomfortable sensation was why he loved disappearing in a big city. In a place like D.C., or Seattle, or Boston, if you didn't stick around too long, no one even noticed you.

When he got outside, Josh went over to his Harley. He shouldn't have come here. He shouldn't have stopped off to see Eric. By now, he could be a hundred miles closer to L.A. and his next job. Staying in Raynes for a couple of weeks could lead to complications, and he was a man who hated complications. But he'd needed to see for himself that Eric was okay. The man had been like a brother to him since their days in the service. Moreover, Eric had always been there for him whenever he needed a friend. It was time to return the favor.

He'd hoped to cheer Eric up, maybe make the hospital stay less painful. So far, Josh was pretty certain he'd cheered Eric up. He'd no more gotten to the hospital tonight before his friend had asked him to come over here and pick up his sister Blair. And how could he refuse? Eric was covered with an assortment of casts, and held together by gizmos and gadgets. It was impossible for Josh to say no. Though, for a man as banged up as Eric was, he'd been in a fine mood once Josh had agreed to his request.

Glancing at the door to the auditorium, Josh ran a tired hand over his chin. He was being set up. He could feel it. He just didn't know what for. But any armchair detective could spot a plot this obvious. First Eric's cheerful request, then the open-mouthed stares in the theater, and finally, the almost laughable "ask him" nonsense of a few minutes ago.

Oh, yeah. It was a setup. And pretty Blair Collins was smack dab in the middle of it.

When the outside door to the auditorium opened, Josh watched with interest as the people filed out. Most of them shot him a curious glance, a couple stared, and the blond even gave him a flirty little wave.

But no one said a word. Josh smiled and shook his

head. *Setup. Big time.* By the time Blair came down the front steps, he'd braced himself for whatever bomb she wanted to drop.

"Hi," she said, stopping a few feet away from him. Even in the dim light of the parking lot, he could tell she was nervous.

"Hi, again." He picked up the spare helmet off the seat of his bike and handed it to her. "Eric told me you needed a ride to the hospital."

Blair looked at the helmet in her hands, avoiding his gaze. "Yes. Eric was driving my car when he had the accident, and it was totaled. I haven't gotten a new one yet."

"Must have been a terrible wreck."

With a nod, Blair looked up at him. "Awful. We're lucky Eric wasn't killed."

"He said he had a blow out, lost control, and smashed into a tree."

Blair leaned forward and said in a conspiratorial tone, "Actually, according to witnesses, he swerved to avoid a squirrel, and that's what caused the wreck."

With Blair this close, Josh could smell her tantalizing perfume. Between the enticing scent and her teasing smile, he felt an unwanted tug of attraction. He looked away, hoping to break the spell. It helped, but only a little.

"Avoiding a squirrel, huh? Sounds like Eric," he said.

Blair stood silently for a moment, her attention again focused on the helmet in her hands. Finally, she said, "I could have asked one of the cast members for a ride to the hospital."

"That's right. Eric said you're rehearsing a play." He grabbed his own helmet and looked at her again. "It's no problem giving you a ride to the hospital."

She was studying him. Up close like this, he could see indecision in her eyes. Feel the hesitation in her stance. *The setup.* Whatever she needed to ask him, he could tell she wasn't thrilled with the idea.

"Something wrong?" he asked, even though he wasn't sure he wanted to hear the answer. *A pretty woman with a problem was bound to be a complication. One he didn't need. Didn't want.*

When she took a hesitant step forward, he knew he was in big trouble. He'd never been good at telling a lady no, and he certainly didn't want to practice on Eric's sister.

"I need to ask you something," she said softly.

The other cast members had left, so the warm June air was quiet except for the occasional sound of a car passing on the street out front. He felt his stomach knot.

"What?" he asked.

"I know this is kind of strange, but . . ."

Strange? She wanted to ask him something strange?

He didn't like the sound of that. "Look, Blair, I'm not—"

"I need a Prince Charming."

There. She'd asked. Feeling like she'd just dropped a fifty-pound cement block, she sighed with relief. She wasn't good at asking for favors. But her back was to the wall, and besides, it did seem almost fortuitous that he'd walked in at the exact moment she'd needed an attractive man.

"Excuse me?" Josh asked.

Blair explained what had happened with Kyle. When she finished, she mentally crossed her fingers. Josh's face gave no clue as to what he was thinking. She tried to encourage him. "It was like you were destined to arrive at that moment."

"Hate to break it to you, Blair, but destiny had nothing to do with this—Eric did. He sent me over tonight."

Blair could tell from Josh's tone that he intended to say no. There had to be *something* she could say to change his mind. Heck, there was a pretty good chance this was why Eric had sent Josh over here in the first place. More than likely, Kyle had gotten his stitches at the same hospital where Eric was staying. The same hospital where nurses fawned over her brother like he was a rock star. Eric had his own personal grapevine around that hospital.

Josh cleared his throat. "Look, about this Prince Charming thing, it's just not something I'm cut out for."

His rueful tone made it clear he was talking about a lot more than the play. She wanted to ask him why he thought that, but it seemed rude to pry. She decided it was best to let the matter go for the moment.

"I understand. We're desperate, so I had to ask." She studied his motorcycle. "Is that what we're taking to the hospital?"

"Yes." He climbed on the bike, steadying it as she got on behind him. It had been years since she'd been on a motorcycle. She'd dated a boy in high school who'd had one, but she didn't remember the seating position being so close. *Yikes.* She tried to relax and stay calm, but when Josh started the bike, she realized it wasn't going to be easy.

"Hold on to me," Josh shouted over the roar of the engine.

"Um. Sure." Gingerly, she slid her arms around his taut waist. She kept her grip loose, but Josh tugged on her arms, tightening up her hold.

"You know how to lean on one of these?" he asked.

"Yes." Thankfully, he wasn't looking at her so he couldn't see the blush she felt warming her face.

He headed toward the hospital. The rumble of the engine and the vibration startled her, and she involuntarily wrapped her arms tighter around him. Her boyfriend in high school had had a much smaller motorcycle—it hadn't been this big or this loud. But as Josh maneuvered through the streets of Raynes, Blair never doubted for a second that he was in complete control.

Sitting this close to him, Blair tried to ignore the rapid beat of her heart. She was acting crazy. There was no reason to get flustered from a simple motorcycle ride, especially when the man in question was Josh Anderson.

If she remembered correctly what Eric had told her, Josh never stayed anywhere long. He did contract computer programming work and went from job to job, never staying in one place for more than a few months.

Just the sort of man Blair had no interest in. So what if he was good-looking? He was a man without roots, and she'd spent her life longing for stability. She finally had it, and someday she knew she'd find the right guy to share it with—someone who wanted the same things out of life that she did.

She'd already had enough heartache. When it became clear that she wanted to settle down in one place, her ex-fiancé, Marshall, had decided he couldn't handle that lifestyle, and jilted her a few days before their wedding. Next time she fell in love, she'd find someone who wanted to stay in one place and raise a fam-

ily. Someone she could love with her whole heart—
which was definitely *not* Josh Anderson.

"You're a rat," Blair said as they walked into Eric's
room.

Josh trailed after her, keeping a safe distance away
from her perfume. The ride over here had been sweet
torment. Feeling her so close had really tested his self-
control.

"Why am I a rat?" Eric had a telltale grin on his
face. If Josh had had any doubts about his friend's
part in this plot, that grin erased them.

"You know why." Blair dropped into the worn plastic chair next to the bed. "You sent poor Josh over to
pick me up knowing full well I'd ask him to be in the
play."

Eric chuckled. Despite the discomfort Josh knew he
was experiencing, he was smiling like he'd just won
the lottery. "Well, maybe I did suspect you could use
Josh's help."

Josh wanted to be angry with Eric, but he couldn't.
The man was a mess, and if this little joke brightened
his day, then Josh could take it.

"Real cute, Eric," Josh said, sitting in the other chair
at the foot of the bed.

"One of the nurses told me about Kyle, so I knew
Blair would need a new Prince Charming. You'll have
fun—"

"Whoa—hold on. I told her no."

Eric's smile faded. "Why'd you say no? It'll be really easy, and you said earlier you were going to stick around for a few days. What's the problem?" Eric asked.

With each passing moment, Josh felt the trap closing around him. Not only didn't he want to be in a play, the thought of being Prince Charming was almost a joke.

"I'm not an actor," Josh said, hoping they'd let it go.

But Eric wasn't through. "You don't have to be. Neither am I, but I said I'd help out. This is a children's play. The audience will be parents and kids. They don't expect perfection."

Josh looked at Blair, who sat expressionless. Even though he knew this play was important to her, he also knew she had a soft spot. If he reasoned with her, he sensed she'd understand.

"Blair, look, I'm sorry. But I'm not the Prince Charming type." He could see the sympathy in her pale hazel eyes.

"You don't have to slay a dragon or anything," she said softly. "All you have to do is dance with Cinderella during the ball scene and then kiss her at the end of the play. It's actually one of the smaller parts."

"She could really use your help," Eric added. "I'd take it as a personal favor."

A personal favor. Josh silently groaned. *This from the man who'd done countless favors for him.* He cleared his throat, trying again. "Look, I don't think—"

"Come on, Josh. It's no big deal. All you have to do is stand around and look pretty," Eric said. Although Josh admired his friend's loyalty to his sister, he would've appreciated it more if it hadn't been at his expense.

He saw no way out. He owed Eric. The man had always been there for him during hard times. He couldn't refuse; he believed in being there for his friends. So reluctantly, he relented. "Okay, fine. I'll help. But I'm warning you, I'm going to be terrible."

Blair rewarded him with a brilliant smile that acted like a punch to his already wobbly equilibrium. "Thank you, Josh. This means so much to all of us. I promise I'll make it as painless as possible."

"Yeah." A new thought occurred to him. "I won't have to wear tights, will I?"

Blair laughed, and the sweet sound ran over him like warm honey. What had he gotten himself into?

"No. No tights. You wear a regal blue suit," she said. "The color's beautiful. It exactly matches your eyes."

At her compliment, he looked at her. She also seemed surprised by what she said, but she didn't look away.

So she felt the connection between them, too. Not good. He might have had a chance at fighting this attraction if the pull had been one-sided. But now that he knew she also felt it, staying away from her would be nearly impossible.

Distance. What he needed was distance. He'd just make certain he only saw Blair when they were doing the play, and there were lots of other people around.

A pretty nurse appeared in the doorway and flashed a smile at Eric. "Visiting hours are over now. Mr. Collins needs some rest."

That suited Josh just fine. It was past time for him to get out of here. Once he got to Eric's house, maybe things wouldn't look so bad.

He stood and turned to Blair. "I thought I'd drop you off at your place on my way to Eric's house."

A mumble from Eric caught Josh's attention. His friend's expression made the sick feeling in Josh's stomach return.

"About my house," Eric said slowly. "I know I said you could stay there while you're in town, but . . ."

"No big deal. If it's a problem, I'll just go to a hotel."

Blair stepped forward. "There aren't any hotels or motels around Raynes. You'd have to drive forever to find one."

Confused, Josh looked from Blair to Eric and then back to Blair. *What was going on here?*

"So what's the problem?" With a grin to Blair, he added, "I promise I'm housebroken, and I won't steal the silver."

She returned his smile, and once again he realized just how pretty she was . . . and just how much trouble he was in. Distance. He definitely needed distance. The less he saw of Blair Collins, the better off he'd be.

"I trust you, Josh," she said. "The problem is that Eric doesn't have a house."

"An apartment?" he asked hopefully.

From the bed, Eric chuckled, but he didn't say anything.

"Yes, he has an apartment," Blair said. "Well, sort of."

Sort of? Suddenly, Josh knew what Blair was going to say before the words left her mouth.

"He's been staying in the garage apartment at my house. I guess you'll have to stay there, too." She gave him another sweet smile. "I hope you don't mind being neighbors for a couple of weeks."

Chapter Two

"You'll have to forgive the house. I just bought it, and it needs some work," Blair said, glad her voice didn't reflect how jittery the motorcycle ride from the hospital had left her. Without looking at Josh, she climbed off the motorcycle and led the way up the front steps to her house.

"Were you looking for a fixer-upper?" Josh asked, following her to the door.

Blair glanced at him, then unlocked the door. "Not really, but I didn't have a lot of money, and I fell in love with this place. You can't see because it's too dark, but the house has this wonderful gingerbread trim."

"Kind of a Hansel and Gretel thing, huh?" Josh

moved forward until he stood next to her. "You seem to be living in one big fairy tale," he added with a chuckle.

Well, at least he still had a sense of humor. Considering how she and Eric had practically coerced him into acting in the play, she was pleasantly surprised.

"I'm not sure you can equate my life to a fairy tale. To be honest, it's starting to take on a real Stephen King feel."

Blair opened the front door and led the way inside. After she'd turned on a couple of table lamps, she turned to face Josh. He seemed so out of place in her cozy living room with her Queen Anne furniture. The man seemed too large, with his imposing height and broad shoulders.

Josh wandered around the room, his restlessness reminding her of a caged lion. As he walked he studied the room, apparently aware of her scrutiny. "Stephen King? Tell me I'm not going to wake up in the middle of the night and find you in my room holding an ax."

She laughed. "No, I'm not the ax type."

He flashed her a crooked grin that was very appealing. "I didn't think so, but hey, it doesn't hurt to ask."

"I guess not." Moving through the living room, she headed to the side door. Josh probably was anxious to see where he'd be staying.

"I straightened up Eric's apartment yesterday, so it's

in good shape," she said as she headed outside. The warm Texas air brushed her face as she led the way across the back yard to her garage. The apartment upstairs was perfect for visitors, and it was one of the first things she'd renovated when she'd moved into the house.

"Nice night." Josh walked next to her, but abruptly he stopped and drew a couple of deep breaths of night air into his lungs. "You know," he said, his expression unreadable in the dark night, "one of the things I like most about my job is I get to see so many places. Even the night sky seems different wherever you go. I like that."

As an army brat, Blair almost shuddered. She'd hated moving all the time, never able to call any one place home. Things had only gotten worse after her mother died. Then her father had decided Blair needed a female influence and shipped her off to stay with her aunt. Living with her aunt might have been okay if Eric had come with her, but their father had insisted his son stay with him. To this day, Blair associated new places with loneliness.

"Is that why you do contract programming?" she asked when they started walking again. "So you can visit new places?"

"It's part of the reason."

"Part?"

He was silent for a long time before he said, "I'm not the type to settle down."

Blair wasn't sure what he meant by that, but she let the subject drop. Instead, she climbed the stairs leading up to the apartment, unlocked the door, and turned on the overhead light. The apartment was actually a large open area. She'd used furniture to divide the area into a compact living room and dining room. The kitchen was tucked away in the far corner. After moving in, Eric had bought a new refrigerator and a microwave.

"This is nice." Josh tossed a black duffel bag on the couch, then set his laptop computer on the dining room table.

"Thanks. Eric helped." She gave him a quick tour, showing him where the bedroom and bathroom were.

"Eric almost looks like he's settling in," Josh said.

"He is. He plans on staying here until he finds his own place."

"I didn't realize he wanted to live in Raynes," Josh said. "I didn't think Eric would ever settle down."

"Me neither, but people are full of surprises." Blair glanced at Josh, which proved to be a big mistake. Their gazes met and held. She couldn't help wondering about him. *Why did he avoid ties? Avoid staying in one place? The man was a mystery.*

With effort, Blair fought to keep her thoughts on track. Eventually, she broke his gaze. Clearing her throat, she said, "There's plenty of room in the closet for your things. And most of the drawers are empty— Eric's only using the top two."

Josh nodded toward the duffel bag. "This is all I have."

"Oh, right, you don't have much room to carry stuff with you on a motorcycle. Guess you'd topple over if you didn't pack lightly. So do you send for your belongings after you get where you're going?"

She wasn't trying to pry, just making conversation, but her question seemed to bother him. Though he didn't move a single muscle, she felt him tense.

"I have a few things in storage, but I don't usually send for them," he said, glancing away.

As more awkward seconds ticked by, Blair had an increasingly strong urge to escape the small apartment. Deciding to give into that urge, she edged toward the door. "How about something for dinner? Rehearsing always makes me hungry."

Josh had been looking at a couple of pictures on the wall, but he turned to face her just as she neared the door. A smile tugged on the corner of his mouth, and she could tell he knew she was fleeing.

"Sounds good," he said.

As he followed her down the steps, she asked, "Where do you live when you're working?"

"My clients provide me with a furnished place to stay."

Wow. She'd hate that. But Josh's life wasn't any of her business. Some people enjoyed moving. "Do you like what you do?"

"It's a terrific challenge."

Blair smiled. Josh was a lot like her brother. Eric could never walk away from anything challenging. "Eric says you're very good at it, too."

"I have fun."

Because of her attraction to Josh, or maybe in spite of it, curiosity ate at Blair. She wanted to know more about him. Eric had told her only a few things about his friend, and she sensed Josh had more than a few secrets in his past.

Just like you do.

Blair pushed the thought aside, which wasn't difficult to do with Josh so close. When she reached the bottom of the stairs, she turned to face him. Floundering for something to say, she asked, "Don't you ever wish you could go to your own home every night?"

"No," he finally answered, his tone flat. "Never."

Blair was a woman surrounded by things, Josh thought when he followed her back into the house. She didn't have expensive things, just sentimental items. In the living room, little figurines lined the mantle, interspersed around pictures of Eric and an older couple, probably her parents. Josh leaned closer to get a good look at the figures. Leprechauns and unicorns. "These are interesting."

She smiled. "I like whimsy in my life," she said before she headed toward the kitchen.

Josh followed her, studying the house as he went. Blair kept the rooms neat and organized, but it didn't take an expert to see she had her work cut out for her. The house was indeed a fixer-upper, although once completed it would be beautiful. Whoever built it had put a lot of thought into the details, especially the molding and trim.

"So tell me about this play," Josh said, joining Blair in the kitchen. He skidded to a stop when he caught sight of the lime green and burnt orange cabinets. *Wow.* He'd had nightmares that weren't as disturbing as this kitchen. Still, Blair had managed to soften the effect with white appliances, and she'd given the room flair by placing more personal items around. *Yep, Blair Collins was firmly planted in her home.* This woman liked to nest—his polar opposite.

"The play should be a lot of fun, and it won't take up much of your time. We're rehearsing every night this week, and our first performance is on Friday evening. Then we have another performance on Saturday, a couple more rehearsals next week to keep us fresh, and then the remaining two performances are on the following Friday and Saturday. Josh, I really appreciate you taking the part of Prince Charming," Blair said. "It won't be difficult."

Josh leaned against the doorway. "Except so far, the two guys who previously signed up to play Prince Charming both ended up getting hurt. This play sounds sort of dangerous."

She smiled at his teasing. "It's not dangerous if you're a careful driver, and you don't catch baseballs with your face."

"No problem there." His good intentions about squashing his attraction to Blair wavered when she opened the refrigerator door. The light from inside highlighted her profile, the classic lines of her face, the length of her throat. *Resisting Blair was going to be difficult.* She was not only pretty, she also had an appealing, warm personality.

Talk about a dangerous combination.

"What would you like for dinner?" Blair asked.

"Since you're letting me stay here, I'll fix dinner," he said, anxious to do something other than stare at her.

He expected an argument, but Blair shrugged and moved away from the refrigerator. "Sounds good. I'm not much of a cook."

Josh rooted around the refrigerator until he found the makings for sandwiches and a salad. They worked together making the meal, but soon the conversation lagged and Josh sensed she was as jumpy as he was.

By the time they sat at the small kitchen table, attraction cracked between them like electricity.

"Do you mind satisfying my curiosity about something?"

Josh swallowed a sip of his soda. "Guess not. What?"

"Why did you finally agree to help us with the play?" Blair had stopped eating and sat watching him closely.

Josh saw no reason to pretend. "The bottom line is I owe your brother a lot, so I'm doing it for him." He didn't intend his words to sound harsh, but they did, and the faint smile on Blair's face faded.

"You don't have to help if you don't want to. I can find someone else," she said.

"If you could have, I'm sure you would have." Leaning back in his chair, he studied her. When she met and held his gaze, he forced himself to look away, not wanting to get tangled in her spell.

"It's no big deal. I don't mind," he finally said.

"Well, you're a nice man to help."

Nice? She thought he was nice? That was a first. He'd been rowdy as a kid, wild as a teen, and a hardhead in the Army. These days, he was good at his job, and most people probably respected him. But no one had ever called him nice. That word made him uncomfortable. Nice was settled. Nice was comfortable.

"No offense, but I'm not nice. Nice makes me feel

like I'm your second cousin here to take you to the prom." He leaned forward, wanting to stress the point. "A nice guy would have agreed to help without being shoved into it by his best friend."

"Is that what Eric did? Shove you into agreeing?"

"In his own way, yeah. Like I said, I owe him, and he knows it."

"Does that bother you?"

Josh smiled. "No. I admire his resourcefulness."

Blair laughed, and the sound tensed every muscle in his body. This woman had the uncanny ability to really get under his skin. Until tonight, he hadn't thought that was possible, but something about Blair pulled at him, and he knew if he wasn't careful he could end up in real trouble. Blair struck him as the marriage-and-children type. That wasn't his style. He came from a family where divorce was common, so he avoided women who were interested in forever. He didn't want to end up like his parents, both of whom had left behind a trail of broken marriages.

"Well, despite what you've said, I still think you're nice." After a slight pause, she added, "But I should probably warn you that not everyone in the play is . . . nice."

He didn't really care if the people were nice or not. But his gut told him this play definitely had a chance of turning into a royal mistake. Still, he owed Eric.

And he knew he'd been through worse things—the Army hadn't exactly been a cakewalk.

"I'll keep my guard up." He studied Blair. Now *she* was really nice. All she'd done tonight was worry about others—about the play and the hospital that would profit from it. And she'd worried about *him*. Josh couldn't remember the last time someone had worried about him. It felt . . . odd. Pushing the unwanted feeling aside, he deliberately changed the subject. "Do you like living in Raynes?"

An almost blissful look crossed her face. "I absolutely love it. I never belonged anywhere until I found this town."

"You and Eric were Army brats, right?"

She nodded, her brown hair brushing her shoulders. "Yes. You know the story—all we did was move, and every time I made friends or felt settled, we were off to another base. I hated it. I wanted a place I could call home." She hesitated, then added, "Especially after my mom died."

"Eric told me you went to live with your aunt."

The light seemed to fade from her eyes. "That's right. My dad thought I needed a female's influence. Unfortunately, my aunt would have preferred to get malaria than be saddled with a teenager."

No wonder she'd wanted roots. When he'd been a kid, he'd loved his small town. He'd known everyone, had friends from birth, felt like the place was his. Then after his parents' divorce, everything had changed, and he no longer felt wanted in the place he'd once loved.

"Why'd you pick Raynes?" he asked.

She tensed. He didn't know what painful memory he'd stepped in, but he sensed she wasn't going to tell him anymore than she'd already shared.

"I used to live in Dallas, and one afternoon I happened upon Raynes and fell in love." She paused for so long, he thought she wasn't going to add anything else. But eventually, she said, "Some stuff happened to make me want to relocate, so I came here about a year ago. I find Raynes comforting."

He wanted to ask why she'd left Dallas, why she'd been seeking comfort, but he didn't. Life had taught him to respect the pain of others, so he backed off. Instead, he picked up the dirty dishes and carried them to the sink.

"What about you? Where do you live when you're not working?" she asked behind him.

"No place. When I have time off, I travel."

"You don't have a permanent home?" she asked.

He ran warm water in the sink. "Nope. Just a mailbox back in Oklahoma and a few things in storage."

"But there must be *someplace* you'd like to live."

"No." He didn't want to discuss his lifestyle. No way a woman who collected figurines of leprechauns could understand how he felt. She'd just told him how much she loved living in a small town, while he'd spent years getting away from one.

"No small town or big city?" she prompted.

"No place." When he did turn around, she stood a couple of feet from him, her expression intense, her gaze sympathetic.

"Look, Blair," he said. "I'm not the settling-down type. I like to move around. Discover new places." He smiled, trying to lighten the mood. "Some of us don't plan to put roots down until we're buried six feet under."

Blair returned his smile. "My folks were like that. But they still always had houses. And they had a family. Don't you want those things? Don't you want to find some place you can live permanently?"

He could tell she wasn't going to drop this. Obviously, Eric hadn't told her anything about his past, and Josh knew he could leave it that way. He could give her a flippant answer like he gave everyone else, but somehow, he couldn't do that to Blair. Maybe it was the concern in her eyes, or the fact that he was tired, but whatever it was, he told her the truth.

"Forever isn't in my blood, Blair."

Blair's eyes were gritty with fatigue the next morning. After showering and dressing for work, she headed downstairs for some much-needed coffee. As she looked out her kitchen window, she couldn't help wondering if Josh was still asleep. Probably not. He wouldn't have spent half the night awake wondering about her the way she had about him.

The man was a puzzle to her. After his pronouncement that forever wasn't in his blood, their conversation had dwindled to nothing. He'd made it clear he considered the subject closed. Respecting his privacy, she'd let the matter drop, but she couldn't help wondering what had happened to him in the past. Naturally, Eric knew the answers, but she wouldn't ask her brother. No, if she wanted to understand Josh better, she had to find the answers herself.

But she wouldn't go looking for them. Last night had shown her how different their beliefs were, not to mention their future plans. Blair now understood that the less she knew about Josh, the better off she would be. He could stay in Eric's apartment, and she'd be friendly to him, but that was it. She wasn't about to fall for a man like Josh.

Plus, she already had more than enough to think about. First, she had a business to grow. Then there was the house. Josh had been very polite last night, but Blair knew she had a ton of work to do. Finally, there was the play. She'd made a commitment to help, and she'd do everything she could to make it a success.

No sense getting distracted at this point by a handsome man—she'd fallen in that trap before. Marshall had seemed perfect for her, and she'd mistakenly believed he wanted the same things out of life she did. But he hadn't understood how much she needed to settle in one place, somewhere she could form ties with the people around her.

Funny how the thought of her ex-fiancé's desertion no longer shot pain through her. Time really did heal all wounds. When Marshall had walked out on her right before the wedding, she figured that understanding men wasn't her forte. She honestly believed that Marshall wanted to settle down and start a family. But instead, when offered a slightly better job that called for frequent moves, he'd chosen it over her. But she was smarter now, so she'd steer a wide detour around Josh Anderson and save herself some heartache in the process.

Before leaving the kitchen, Blair turned off the coffee maker and crossed to the living room. Theresa would be here in a few moments to give her a ride to work. Thankfully, this would be the last ride Blair would need. This afternoon she was leaving work early to buy a new car.

Before locking the front door, Blair headed down the steps to retrieve the newspaper. Her delivery person always left it right by the street, but oddly enough, this morning it was sitting on the top step.

Instantly, Blair knew Josh must have put the paper there. Glancing around the yard, she saw no sign of him, and his motorcycle sat where he'd parked it last night.

So where was he? Blair walked down the driveway. When she reached the sidewalk, she looked up and down the block. Finally, she spotted him. Jogging down the street wearing shorts and a T-shirt, he was a sight to make a woman's heart beat faster. Blair couldn't stop herself from watching him run and was so caught up in the sight that it took her a minute to notice he stopped briefly at each house. Smiling, she realized what he was doing. Josh was picking the papers up in front of each house, and with a skilled arm, tossing them lightly onto the front porch. She'd give him this—he had great aim.

Theresa pulled up just as Josh was almost back to the house. Blair walked over to Theresa's car, but before she could get in her friend climbed out and turned to watch Josh.

"Now *that's* what I call an early morning vision," Theresa said, shading her eyes against the early morning sun. "And look—he's such a nice guy. He's throwing the papers up to the houses. This man definitely has Prince Charming written all over him."

Except he doesn't think so, Blair thought as she watched Josh approach the front of her house.

"Morning, ladies." Josh walked over to where they stood.

Theresa took two steps forward, stopping to block his path. "Where'd you learn to toss a paper like that?"

Josh shrugged. "I used to play football in high school."

"A quarterback," Theresa said with a wink to Blair. "I should have guessed it. You have the look of a hometown hero."

Josh extended his hand and introduced himself.

"Oh, sugar, I remember you from last night." Theresa shot another quick glance at Blair, then returned her attention to Josh. "So are you joining our little play?"

"Yeah. I don't have much else to do while I'm in town." He looked at Blair, his blue eyes intense in the early morning sun. "I can give you a ride to work."

Theresa giggled. "Now wouldn't that be a sight? Blair coasting to work in her nice suit on the back of a Harley."

As Josh studied her suit, with its knee-length A-line skirt, Blair forced herself not to blush—not even when his gaze lingered.

"I see what you mean," he said. After a prolonged moment, his gaze met hers. Blair felt her rapid heartbeat increase its pace.

"Theresa's giving me a ride to work this morning. And this afternoon, I'm going to buy a car," Blair said.

"Why don't you go with her?" Theresa shot a conspiratorial look at Blair. "I'm sure she'd appreciate your advice."

Blair frowned at her friend. *Why was it that married people always felt they had to fix up the rest of the world?* She turned to Josh. "I already know what kind of car I want."

"But Josh might have fun helping," Theresa said. "He can't spend the whole day at the hospital visiting Eric. Those cute nurses won't let him." When she finished speaking, she flashed a triumphant grin at Blair.

Blair could read the hesitation in Josh's expression and wished she knew what he was thinking.

"She seems to have it covered. I don't think she needs me to tag along," he said.

"Don't be silly." Theresa's grin widened. "She'd love the company."

No two ways about it, Blair really needed to have a heart-to-heart with Theresa. Although her friend meant well, backing Josh into a corner like this wasn't nice. But since Theresa and Josh stood looking at her, Blair didn't have a choice. She had to agree.

"You can come with me if you want to," Blair said half-heartedly. Spending time with Josh wasn't wise— the attraction between them was simply too strong.

"How can you turn down Blair's gracious invitation?" Theresa asked, her smile far too smug. "Blair, honey, why don't you run upstairs and grab some casual clothes to wear while you're car shopping this afternoon? That way, when Josh comes to pick you up on his motorcycle, you won't have to worry about your skirt."

Blair sighed. She should take the safe course of action and politely refuse Josh's help. Unfortunately, Theresa would probably devise a new argument, and Blair really didn't want to stand in her driveway arguing all morning with her best friend.

"I'll just go change my clothes," Blair finally said. Resigned, she walked back into the house, making a mental note to tell Theresa to stop matchmaking. It wasn't going to work. Not this time.

Chapter Three

Whenen Blair rejoined Theresa and Josh, she was wearing tailored navy slacks and a cream-colored blouse. At least now she could ride on Josh's motorcycle.

Theresa was laughing when Blair walked up to them. At Blair's questioning look, Theresa said, "Josh just told me the most hysterical story about a llama. He's sure seen more than his fair share of the world."

"Seems that way. Well, we'd better get to work." Blair smiled at Josh, and ignored the little flip-flop her heart did when he flashed a crooked grin back. "My phone number at work is on Eric's refrigerator," she said, finding it difficult to concentrate when he looked at her with those intense blue eyes of his.

"Thanks, but I'm sure I won't need to call. I'll probably head over to the hospital in a while and visit Eric."

Nervously, Blair tucked a stray strand of hair behind her ear. "I'm sure he'd love that. He feels well enough to get bored."

"Great." With a quick goodbye, Josh headed toward the garage.

"Now *that's* what I call good-looking," Theresa whispered.

Blair didn't even pretend not to know what her friend meant. Josh was incredibly handsome, with his classic features. Without thinking, she watched him disappear around the back of the house.

"Well, I'll be. You like him," Theresa teased as they walked over to her car.

Snapping out of her reverie, Blair glanced at Theresa. "No, I don't. But I will admit he's attractive."

"Attractive? Right, in the way that Bill Gates is comfortable financially. Come on, Blair. Josh is gorgeous."

"But he's all wrong for me." Blair slipped into the passenger seat and fastened her seatbelt, considering the subject closed. She had nothing in common with Josh; they wanted different things in life. If her experience with Marshall had taught her nothing else, she had learned that to make a relationship last, you have to find someone who is similar to you.

Opposites might attract, but they didn't stay together long.

Josh stared out the kitchen window in Eric's apartment, his mind a million miles away. From this vantage point, he could clearly see the back of Blair's house. Not that seeing her house was a good thing— it only served to remind him how cautious he needed to be around his new neighbor. He found himself drawn to Blair, and he was spending far too much time thinking about her.

Which no doubt explained why he was so tense this morning. Even his jog hadn't soothed his nerves, and he couldn't shake the feeling that he was getting himself too deeply involved in Blair's life. First by joining the play, then by agreeing to stay in Eric's apartment, now by helping her look for a new car. He was getting pulled in, and he needed to be careful. He could end up getting hurt. Or worse, Blair could end up getting hurt.

Refusing to even consider the possibility, he headed to take a shower. After jogging three miles, he certainly needed one and hopefully it would relax him.

He showered and dressed quickly, wanting to head over to the hospital and visit with Eric. Maybe seeing his friend would get rid of this nagging feeling he had. With any luck, after his visit, he'd be able to put everything in perspective. Then by the time he picked up Blair this afternoon, he'd be in control again.

As long as he kept his mind off of Eric's baby sister, this visit would work out fine.

"This 'Vette looks perfect for you."

Blair glanced at Josh, who was leaning against a shiny red sports car, looking too handsome for words in his blue jeans and T-shirt. His aviator sunglasses blocked the devilment she knew she'd see in his blue eyes.

"I think I'll pass on the Corvette. But thanks anyway." She turned back to the small, brown-gold sedan she'd been considering. "This one is nice."

Josh came over to stand next to her. This close, she could smell the woodsy cologne he used. "What do you think?"

"You're kidding, right?" He pulled open the door and studied the dash. "I've seen hearses with more pizazz."

He was right. The car was boring, especially when the other cars on the lot seemed to be either sporty or elegant. But she needed something reliable that wouldn't break her budget.

"I'm not interested in pizazz." She refused to look at Josh. He'd taken off his sunglasses, and she knew looking at him would be distracting. "I want a dependable car."

"Dependable doesn't mean it can't be fun," he pointed out.

Blair studied the sedan. It certainly didn't look fun.

"Let's check it over." Josh reached around her and popped the hood. After walking to the front of the car, he looked at the engine. Blair came to stand next to him.

"This may come as a surprise, but I do know how an engine works," she said, humor lacing her voice. "I even know how to change the oil."

He turned toward her, a smile on his handsome face. "I never thought for a minute you didn't. I just wanted to take a look. Did you expect me to make a sexist comment?"

"I guess. I'm used to men assuming there are a lot of things I can't do."

"Does Eric treat you that way?"

"He used to, but not anymore. I think I may have finally broken him of his bad habits, but it took a while."

Blair watched as Josh ran his hand through his hair. The sun highlighted the strands, and she curved her fingers into her palms to keep herself from reaching out for him. What was it about Josh that made her act like a kid in a candy store?

His look was direct. "So who made you feel dumb, a boyfriend?"

Truthfully, she was really sorry she'd started this

discussion, but she didn't want him thinking she didn't know the front of a car from the back.

"Let's just say my father had, actually he still has, a rather narrow opinion of what women should and shouldn't do."

Josh gave her a rueful smile. "Yeah, parents have a way of making their expectations known."

"Your parents did that too, huh?"

He hesitated for several seconds before he said, "Yeah. They let me know what they thought, and since they seldom agreed with each other, it made life confusing for me. But that's ancient history."

When he let the conversation drop without further explanation, Blair knew he didn't want to talk about this any more than she did. Deciding to change the subject, she leaned over and studied the engine. Although this model car might be reliable, she wanted to make certain this particular one was all right. "The engine looks good, but it's what I can't see that worries me. I'd want to have a mechanic inspect it closely."

She started to move away from the car to find a salesperson, but Josh stopped her by placing his hand lightly on her arm. As happened every time he touched her, a tingle danced across her skin.

"Forget the car for a second," he said. "Your dad really made you feel there were things you couldn't do just because you're female?"

"Yes." Honesty forced her to add, "He was almost forty when I was born, so it was the way he was raised. You know, believing women couldn't do certain things."

"Such as?"

"Lots of things." She turned her attention back to the car, not wanting to dwell on her childhood. "I'm really starting to like this car."

Josh snorted. "Yeah, and I'm hoping a meteorite lands on me." He followed her as she walked around the car, studying it closely. Finally, he said, "So, considering your problems with your dad, why are you doing *Cinderella*? Isn't that like the ultimate put-down of women? Cinderella doesn't tell the stepmother and stepsisters to take a hike, she just lets them walk all over her. And she only manages to get to the ball because a fairy godmother makes it happen. Not to mention that the reason the prince falls for Cinderella is because she's a knockout, not because she's a nice person. Which, come to think of it, means the prince is kind of a doofus, too."

By the time he finished speaking, Blair was laughing. "It's not *that* bad."

He cocked one black brow. "Yes, it is."

She laughed again. "Well, my version isn't that bad."

"Your version?"

"I've made some minor adjustments to the play."

Josh took a couple of steps forward until he stood next to her. He was several inches taller than she was, so she had to tip her head to look at his face. "What kind of adjustments? You're not going to have me out there begging Cinderella to kill a mouse for me, are you?"

Blair was fighting back her humor when her gaze met his. Attraction zinged between them, and her stomach did a little flip-flop. Out of the blue, she couldn't help wondering what it would feel like to kiss him.

Yikes. Pulling her thoughts back from that dangerous direction, she said, "I promise Prince Charming isn't mocked, but I do make certain the audience understands a few things . . ." Her voice trailed off when Josh took another step forward.

"What kinds of things?"

Blair struggled to keep track of the conversation. Josh was so close, he almost brushed against her. But he didn't have her trapped. She could slip around him if she wanted to—except she didn't want to.

"Oh, like how Cinderella has to become brave and learn to believe in herself in order to change her life," Blair said.

Her words seemed to catch his attention. His gaze moved from her eyes to her mouth. "So does she learn that lesson?"

"I think she does, or at least as much as any of us do."

Josh stood there, so close, and yet in some ways, he seemed so far away. Finally, he took a couple of steps back. While Blair struggled to regain her composure, a salesman in a bright yellow jacket came over to them.

"Can I help you folks?"

With effort, Blair turned her attention back to the car. "I'm interested in this sedan," she said, glad her voice had lost the husky, wistful sound it had earlier.

The salesman smiled broadly then launched into an ornate description of the car's positive points. Blair kept her gaze firmly off Josh and forced herself to pay attention to the car. She did fairly well, even managing to ask the salesman a few questions. She may have glanced once or twice at Josh, but that was all. Unfortunately, each time she did glance at him, he was frowning at the car as if it had done something to offend him. So the car wasn't flashy or fun. It did seem to have everything she was looking for—dependability, good mileage, wonderful safety features. Yet when the salesman suggested a test drive, she hesitated.

"I'd like to think about it some more," she said evasively. The salesman took her rejection in stride. "No problem. Are there any other cars you'd like to look at?"

Glancing up, she found Josh watching her intently. He'd been right, and she knew it. The car lacked pizazz. And just because she was looking for something dependable didn't mean she was dead. Deep down, she suspected her change of heart might have something to do with Josh. Okay, so the Corvette in the next aisle over was too wild for her, but now that she thought it over, she did want something fun to drive. *Oh, nothing dangerous or fancy. Just something a little more sporty. A little more adventurous.*

Unable to resist, she turned to the salesman. She gave him the amount she was looking to spend, asked if he had any moderately priced sport cars, and then added impulsively, "And do you have anything in red?"

He'd led her astray, Josh realized as he followed Blair to the high school auditorium for rehearsal a couple of hours later. He hadn't led a woman astray since . . . well, maybe ever. Even as a teenager, he couldn't remember ever having that effect.

But he knew without a doubt Blair would have bought the sedan if he hadn't been there. In his opinion, the snazzy little red Mustang she'd bought suited her better. She might think of herself as sedate and practical, but she had adventure in her soul. It might be well-hidden, but it was there.

Which, if he wasn't careful, could get him in trouble.

They pulled up in front of the auditorium. Josh parked his motorcycle next to Blair's new car and took off his helmet. They'd been pretty lucky to get everything done on the car today. After a short test drive, Blair had pronounced the car perfect and used her insurance money to pay for it.

Judging from the ear-to-ear grin on her face when she got out of the car, Blair was thrilled with her choice.

"I'm so excited. I can't believe I have a CD player and power windows and cruise control." She came over to Josh, still grinning. "I just *love* this car. Thank you for talking me out of the sedan."

She leaned up and gave Josh a hug, which surprised him. For a moment, he hesitated. Then, unable to resist, he loosely wrapped his arms around her.

From the way Blair stiffened in his arms, Josh suspected Blair hadn't really intended to hug him. She'd been caught up in her excitement. But now that he had her in his arms, caution seemed to be melting faster than an ice cube on a summer's day.

Blair made a slight move, and Josh relaxed his hold. He was reluctant to let her go. He wanted to keep her close, to savor the sensations rushing through him that made rational thought difficult. He kept thinking less about what was the *right* thing to do and more about what he *wanted* to do.

When Blair glanced up at him, he could tell she was struggling with the same confusing feelings as he was. Leaning toward her, he said, "Blair?"

He wasn't sure if he was asking her permission or questioning what was happening between them. But common sense had deserted him, so when Blair rose up on her toes, he bent his head and met her lips with his own.

Her kiss tasted of heaven, of promise. Quickly, the gentle kiss ignited like straw touched by a match. Emotions he didn't want to feel zapped through him like lightening, leaving him shaken. But he didn't move away. Instead, the kiss went on and on until the sound of a car on the road in front of the auditorium acted like a bucket of ice water on his heated brain.

Reluctantly, Josh dropped his arms from around her. For a moment, they looked at each other. Then when the car turned into the parking lot, they moved apart and headed inside. Glancing at Blair, Josh felt a connection he couldn't remember ever feeling with a woman. This was not good . . . not good at all.

He wasn't the right type for small towns and families. That wasn't his style. He'd been worried about this trip turning messy, and kissing Blair was one sure way of guaranteeing a mess. Blair was sweet, but she also wanted a life in this small town. Without her even saying so, he knew what that meant. She wanted a home, a husband she could count on, children to love.

So he had to make certain he didn't lead her astray any more. He had to fight the chemistry bubbling between them. It was the only solution, and it was the only fair thing to do. For both of them.

When they got inside the auditorium, Blair introduced him to the other cast members. He was shaking hands with the man playing the King, Bob Julian, when the cold-looking blond woman he'd spotted the day before came down the aisle.

"I have had the most awful day," she said loudly as she joined the group. "Absolutely nothing has gone right, starting with . . ." She stopped talking when she noticed him. Instantly, her face transformed into a flirty smile and an almost savage gleam settled in her pale blue eyes. Josh avoided eye contact, but it did no good. The woman was locked on him like a heat-seeking missile. When she reached his side, she stood so close he could feel the warmth from her body.

"Hello, there," she said. "I'm Leigh Donnelly. Cinderella. Since you're here, I guess you'll be my Prince Charming."

Josh gave her a polite smile, wanting to keep things friendly without giving her any ideas. "Josh Anderson."

"I know. We almost met last night. It's really nice

of you to help with my play. Did Blair tell you that all the money goes to the hospital?"

"Yeah. I think it's a great idea." He shot a quick look at Blair, but she was now talking with Theresa. "Blair tells me you organize this event every year."

"Yes." Leigh shifted subtly, her movement bringing her even closer to him. Before he could move away, she wrapped her hand around his arm and squeezed. "I get the feeling you and I are going to get along great."

Said the spider to the fly. Josh took a deliberate step away from Leigh. He didn't want to make her mad, but he didn't plan on being the main guest at any party this lady had planned.

"I'm sure we will," he said, not meaning it in the least. He glanced at Blair and then back at Leigh. *Talk about the devil and the deep blue sea. Whoever had said that big cities were more dangerous than small towns had never been to Raynes, Texas.*

"She's acting like he's a brand new toy you just bought her," Theresa complained, looking at Leigh and Josh.

Blair nodded. If Leigh got any closer to Josh she'd become another layer of his skin. Glancing away, Blair deliberately focused her attention on the script, not liking the picture the two of them made. Not that she had any claim on Josh. Okay, they'd shared a phenomenal kiss, which had been a mistake. She shouldn't have kissed him. She figured she'd temporarily lost her mind after buying her new car—that had to be the reason. Why else would she kiss Josh, knowing he was completely wrong for her?

"Well, they certainly look like Cinderella and Prince Charming," Theresa commented dryly. "Must be nice to be so good-looking. Life is probably a snap to people like those two."

The trace of bitterness in her friend's voice made Blair look at her. "You really think so? I don't know. Leigh doesn't seem all that happy to me."

"She's rich."

"But lonely," Blair pointed out.

Theresa chuckled. "Not for long, from the looks of things. Leigh keeps trying to wrap around Josh like a vine around a post."

Blair glanced back at the couple. They did look cozy, but it was difficult to tell from this distance if the attraction was mutual. Leigh stood next to Josh, and although her hand was on his arm, he made no move to touch her. In fact, as Blair watched, he took a step away from Leigh.

Maybe Cinderella wouldn't get Prince Charming after all.

Deciding it was time to get down to business, Blair found a spare copy of the script for Josh to study while the others started rehearsal. From the front of the stage, Blair monitored a variety of things: the actors, the lighting, and the props. When the dance scene between Prince Charming and Cinderella started, Blair couldn't help but groan. Josh was doing a fairly good job playing Prince Charming, especially considering he'd had almost no time to study his lines. The only problem was he kept frowning at Leigh rather than looking dazzled.

Blair rubbed her throbbing temples. This wasn't going well. She decided to see what she could do to help Josh out.

"Leigh, please don't dance so close to Josh. When you're both in costume, dancing like that will wrinkle your dress and his uniform."

"Not to mention embarrass the audience," Bob Julian muttered.

Leigh stopped and looked at Blair, a half-smile on her flawless face. "I danced with all my husbands like this. *They* never complained."

"Just cut it out, Leigh," Blair said, not missing the silent thanks Josh sent her way. She released a pent up breath when Leigh gave in and moved a respectable distance from Josh, but Blair suspected it was only a temporary reprieve. Although Leigh wasn't truly malicious, she did have a fairly renowned weakness for gorgeous men. Josh more than qualified as gorgeous. Sure, he was perfectly capable of handling Leigh himself, but Blair wasn't going to sit idly by while Leigh or anyone else made a cast member uncomfortable.

When the dance sequence was finally over, the lighting dimmed. Josh and Leigh sat on a fake brick wall. As they said their lines, Blair listened closely. This was one of the places in the script where she'd made a few small changes. She had the characters talk to each other and share some experiences, so the subtle message went out to the audience that these two people were more than a rich man and a beautiful woman. Blair wanted, if possible, to make them look a little more like real people falling in love. A few times Josh forgot his lines, but overall the scene went well.

After the conversation, the clock started to strike midnight. Leigh ran off the side of the stage, followed by Josh. She was supposed to reappear at the top of a short flight of stairs leading down the right side of the stage. As she ran, she would lose one of her silver heels.

But Leigh didn't appear. Neither did Josh. After a minute, Blair stopped the action and went behind the stage to see what the problem was. The staircase was actually a large ladder with one flight of stairs behind the stage leading up, a platform at the top, and another flight of stairs on the other side leading down to the stage. They had borrowed the prop from the high school's pep team, which used it during rallies. It was incredibly sturdy, but Leigh and Josh was standing in

front of it, studying the stairs. At least, Josh was studying them—Leigh's attention seemed focused on her
handsome co-star.

"What's up?" Blair asked, coming to join them.

Frowning, Josh glanced up. "I have some concerns
about this staircase."

Leigh moved around him and came toward Blair.
"Me, too. Josh asked me if I think I can go up the
stairs when I'm wearing that long, heavy costume, and
I'm not sure I can. I have trouble negotiating the stairs
during rehearsal. What will it be like when I'm in the
long dress during the real play? Plus, these stairs look
weak to me."

Since the stairs had been Leigh's idea, her sudden
change of heart surprised Blair. Still, the woman had
a point. The stairs might be dangerous. Blair walked
over and tried to wobble the structure. It didn't budge.

"The stairs seem stable, but I see your point about
running up in a long dress." Blair continued to study
the staircase. "I guess it is a bad idea to have actors
chasing each other on stairs. Someone could slip and
fall."

They hadn't had any problems so far, but who knew
what would happen once the actors were in their costumes. Blair certainly didn't want anyone to get hurt.

When she looked at Josh, his expression hadn't
changed, but she couldn't shake the feeling he was
relieved by her answer.

"Why don't I just chase her across the stage?" he suggested. "That has to be easier on Leigh if she's running and kicking off her shoe at the same time."

By now, most of the cast and crew had joined them. Blair turned to Leigh. "How's that sound to you?"

"I like it. I can run across the stage with Josh chasing me and lose my slipper. Either way we do the scene, I don't think we'll be nominated for a Tony."

The group laughed. While everyone offered their own humorous suggestions for the category they could be nominated in, Blair studied Josh. Had he really been relieved they weren't using the stairs or was her imagination working overtime?

She made a mental note to talk to him about the stairs later. She didn't have the time to get into it now. With effort, she got the actors back on track and continued the rehearsal. Thankfully, there were no more problems until the very end when Leigh and Josh were to kiss.

Leigh practically threw herself at Josh, who was obviously caught off-guard. He barely managed to keep them from falling over when Leigh emphatically wrapped herself around him and kissed him hard. When Josh attempted to pull away from her, Leigh simply placed one hand against the back of his head to try hold him in place, but he pulled away from her.

"Leigh!" Blair exclaimed, "Stop that." She stood and crossed the stage, noticing that Josh looked about ready to snap. He leaned down and said something to Leigh that made her eyes grow wide.

"I was just kidding," Leigh said, almost defensively. "But if you can't take a joke, then fine."

With a flounce, she walked off stage. Blair turned to look at Josh. "I'm so sorry. I had no idea she'd act like this. We could barely get her within speaking distance of Kyle, our previous Prince Charming."

"Don't worry about it. I think she and I now understand each other," Josh said, being a true gentleman about the situation.

"Well, it's unacceptable. No one should be subjected to harassment." Blair could feel her own anger growing. "I don't care who she is, she doesn't have the right to treat you this way."

"Like I said, don't worry about it."

But she couldn't help worrying. Unfortunately, she knew Leigh. The woman wasn't used to the word no. Sure, the play was important, but not so important that Blair would let Leigh hassle Josh.

Even if it meant losing Leigh as a client, Blair had to prevent a repeat of tonight's disaster.

Chapter Four

"You know, I'm willing to take you to a fancier restaurant." Josh studied the indoor playground at Burgerland. Kids squealed and laughed and tumbled around a complicated series of large plastic tubes. "And I'll even spring for something other than a kid's meal."

Blair smiled at him over the gray table. "I like the kid's meal." She held up a small plastic bag. "Plus, this way, I get a toy to take to the children in the hospital."

Odd feelings tried to tug at Josh, but he ignored them. He wasn't going to get all sappy just because Blair was a nice person. He already knew she was nice—she was directing this play, wasn't she? Not to mention, she'd been kind enough to let him stay in Eric's apartment. No question about it, Blair was a very nice person, and nice people did things they'd rather not just because they were nice.

It was that nice quality about her that made him jumpy. He didn't really know if he could handle nice, especially when it was bundled up with a good dose of humor and intelligence and wrapped up in one incredibly pretty package. The more time he spent with her, the more his thoughts kept wandering in all sorts of dangerous directions.

The main reason he'd talked her into going out to dinner tonight after rehearsal was because he didn't want another cozy dinner at her house. Last night had been difficult enough. But now he knew how wonderful she felt in his arms, how she managed to make all intelligent thought evaporate from his mind the second her lips touched his. For the last couple of hours, he'd thought of little else but the kiss they'd shared.

Which told him as clearly as a neon sign that he was standing dead center in a big pile of trouble.

"I'm really sorry about the way Leigh behaved tonight." Blair neatly folded up the paper wrapper from her burger and set in on the red tray. "I'll speak to her tomorrow."

"You need to stop worrying about Leigh." Josh leaned forward, stealing one of her fries from her meal. "I'm a big boy, Blair. I can handle her."

Looking up, Blair frowned at him, then covered his hand where it lay on the table with her own.

"Josh, I can't promise you Leigh won't do the exact same thing again tomorrow night. She's . . . determined about certain things."

Blair looked so upset, Josh had to smile. "I can take care of myself. Besides, most likely Leigh isn't going to give me any more problems."

"How can you be so sure?" Something about his attitude must have caught her attention because her eyes narrowed. "What did you say to Leigh?"

He turned his hand over and brushed his thumb across Blair's palm. She had the softest skin, even her hands.

Pulling his thoughts back from the meandering direction they'd taken, he removed his hand and leaned back in his chair. "Leigh's simply looking for attention."

"You're being awfully understanding about this."

"One of my father's wives was like Leigh. She acted outrageously, mostly so everyone would notice her. It's sad in a way."

Blair looked confused. "*One* of your father's wives? How many has he had?"

"Four. No wait, five." His answer obviously shocked her. Heck, his father's tendency to marry so often shocked him, too. His mother wasn't much better. She was on her third marriage.

"Wow," she said slowly. "Five marriages."

"Yeah. *Wow*. So you see, I've had a little experience dealing with people like Leigh." Boy, was that ever the truth. His father, like Leigh, was always searching for what he called his perfect partner. The only problem was, David Anderson never seemed to find that person.

Josh wasn't surprised when Blair asked the next logical question. "Have you ever been married?"

"No." His laugh was hollow. "I came close once, but thankfully, we both came to our senses. I've watched too many marriages fail to try that myself."

"But you're such a nice man."

There was that word again—*nice*. He had to set her straight about a few things. "I'm not as nice as you keep making me out to be, Blair. Just because I understand Leigh doesn't make me nice. I did tell her if she didn't back off, I'd tell everyone I met in Raynes that she was a terrible kisser. A woman like Leigh enjoys having men find her irresistible. She would hate to have anyone doubt her appeal. I'm not nice—I knew where Leigh's Achilles heel was, and I went for it."

With fascination, he watched Blair process this information. Maybe now she'd understand he wasn't above a dirty trick, which meant he wasn't a nice guy at all.

"You know, I think your idea will work," Blair finally said. "Leigh is very attractive, so the fact that you haven't fallen at her feet probably is a new sensation for her."

Josh crumbled up the wrapper from his burger and put it on the tray. "I don't think Leigh's attractive."

Blair laughed at his words, but once she realized he was serious, she stared at him. "You're kidding, right? She's beautiful."

"If you like her type, which I don't." As soon as the words left his mouth, he regretted them. Mostly because he knew what Blair's next question would be.

"What *is* your type?" she asked softly.

He met and held Blair's gaze. Yeah, sure—he would answer that question right before he disarmed a ticking bomb. He really didn't have a type, or if he did, it was women who didn't expect too much from him. Women who didn't think he was going to stay around forever. Women who didn't want marriage and a family.

Come to think of it, that was probably a perfect description of Leigh. She'd made it clear she was interested in him.

But the idea of dating Leigh didn't interest him. Not in the least. Unfortunately, the only woman he'd had any interest in was Blair, who was all wrong for him. Didn't it figure? Life always seemed to do this to him.

"Just don't worry about Leigh." He knew he hadn't answered Blair's question about the type of women he liked, and he planned on keeping it that way. He emptied the tray in the nearby garbage can, and waited for Blair to join him at the door.

As she walked by him, she met his gaze, a serious expression on her pretty face. Well, what had she expected him to say—that *she* was his type? Because she wasn't. Not at all. In fact, Blair Collins was everything he avoided in a woman. She was sweet, and settled, and probably believed in love that lasted a lifetime. The bottom line was, Blair wanted everything in life he no longer believed in, so even though he knew he'd disappointed her, he didn't say what he knew she wanted to hear.

Because he couldn't.

Blair kept up a non-stop stream of one-sided conversation as they walked to the front door of her house. Cheerfulness had always been her way of hiding disappointment. Stupidly, she did feel disappointed—which was crazy. She didn't want to be Josh's type, and he certainly wasn't hers. She knew that despite the kiss this afternoon, there really wasn't anything between them.

Sure, Josh was handsome. And he was a lot nicer than he gave himself credit for. But a kindergartner could solve this equation—the two of them simply didn't add up.

Well, at least he'd talked her into buying a car she

loved, not a car she thought she should buy. The Mustang was both practical and sporty, and she was so glad she'd bought it.

As she opened the front door, Josh's silence finally got to her. Floundering for a way to bring him back into the conversation, she said, "Why don't you cut through the house? It's the quickest way to the garage."

Josh hesitated, then finally relented. He followed her inside, locking the door behind him. "The play is going well."

"I think so. I want to thank you again for playing Prince Charming. You're very good at it."

He moved farther into the living room and laughed dryly. "Yeah, right. Mostly I just stand around."

Blair walked over and sat in the far corner of the sofa, then tucked her legs under her. She could see Josh debating what to do; stay with her or head to the garage apartment. She really wasn't sure which she wanted him to choose. As much as she'd like to get to know him better, she also realized there was no point. They were oil and water. They had nothing in common.

Still, when he finally sat at the other end of the couch, she felt a little thrill run through her.

"Even with the problems with Leigh, you're a good actor. I think you're going to be a hit with the kids," Blair said.

He laughed at that and seemed embarrassed. "To tell you the truth, I feel like an idiot."

"Why? You're a natural-born Prince Charming," she teased.

He laughed that self-mocking laugh again. "Not me. No way."

How could he say that? From what she'd seen so far, he was a very kind man. And even though she had no idea what had happened in his past to convince him otherwise, she felt compelled to say, "Josh, you're a great guy."

"There are a lot of people who'd disagree with your statement." Despite his words, he flashed her a crooked grin that made her heart slam against her ribs.

Drawn by his gentle tone, she scooted a little closer. Distracted, he rubbed the back of his neck. She could tell he was sorry he'd said anything, but she wanted to understand this complex man. Without thinking, she placed her hand on his arm and said, "It's been my experience that living up to the expectations of other people is a sure way to make yourself miserable."

When he glanced at her hand on his arm, she started to withdraw it, but he stopped her by placing his own hand over hers. It was the second time tonight they touched this way. Warmth ran through Blair at the feel of his skin against hers. Being this close to Josh was not a very wise move. Unfortunately, she never seemed to do the smart thing when it came to him.

"Is that spoken by a lady who learned that lesson the hard way?"

"That's an understatement." She deliberately kept her tone light. "My folks were often less than impressed with my behavior. Lots of times I failed to do what they expected me to do." She surprised herself by confiding this part of her past to him. It also surprised her how little those old memories hurt. Maybe living in Raynes was helping after all. Or maybe she was growing up. Either way, she was happy to finally feel like a success rather than a failure.

"Did that kind of thing happen to you as a kid?" she asked.

Moving his hand off hers, he shifted on the couch to face her. "Nope. I was the perfect child."

"You can't be serious."

Arching one black brow, he studied her. "What do you think?"

A smile tugged on her lips. "I think you were probably a handful. Actually, based on the stories Eric has told me about the two of you in the Army, I *know* you had to be a handful as a kid. No one becomes that rowdy overnight—it takes years of practice."

Josh chuckled at her description, and the heavy mood that had been settling over them dissipated. She was sorry she'd spoiled the opportunity for him to tell her more about himself, but she also knew he probably wouldn't have. A man like Josh didn't open up easily, and despite how unusually close she felt to him, they'd only known each other one day.

"I gave my folks a lot of gray hair, that's for sure," he said.

Smiling, she turned sideways of the sofa. "Oh, really. What kind of stuff did you do?"

Faint lines fanned out from his eyes as he returned her smile. He really was good-looking, especially right now, with a little twinkle of humor in his deep blue eyes. "I did about anything I could get away with. Unfortunately, I broke a few bones trying stuff I shouldn't have."

"You broke bones?"

"Yeah. A lot of them when I jumped out of my uncle's barn when I was seven."

"Oh no. Were you badly hurt?"

"I spent a few months wearing casts. For Halloween that year, I went as myself," he said with a laugh.

Compassion rushed through Blair for the little boy he'd been. Along with compassion, she felt downright fear at the thought of a child jumping from a barn. "You're lucky you didn't kill yourself. Were you up very high?"

"Yeah."

Suddenly, comprehension dawned on Blair: *the stairs at rehearsal.* He had been so relieved when she'd decided they didn't need to use them. Josh had jumped out of a barn as a kid and was clearly uneasy around heights.

But she didn't ask—men were funny about such things. Blair decided to keep her theories to herself. When she looked up, he wore his trademark crooked grin, the twinkle in his eyes impossible to resist.

"Bet you're not surprised that I don't like heights," he said.

"Oh, yes. I didn't realize . . . I never thought . . ." She waved one hand in the air, at a loss for what to say. "I'm sorry about the stairs."

"They weren't that bad," he assured her. "But ever since the accident, I worry about other people falling. I know I could have killed myself, and I really think those stairs are dangerous for Leigh to run up in her long costume." He leaned toward Blair and with a small smile asked, "Disappointed in me?"

Slowly Blair shook her head. She wasn't surprised he didn't like heights. In fact, she couldn't remember ever meeting a person who didn't have some fear. Heights, planes, small spaces. Something. What amazed her was that he had confided in her; he trusted her enough to tell her the truth.

"No. I agree it isn't safe having you and Leigh running up and down those stairs. One of you could fall."

"It's a definite possibility," Josh said.

Blair studied him, filled with admiration. She had never met a man who overwhelmed her the way Josh did. It was the way he dealt with people, the way he addressed everyone around him with respect. The cast members were really taken with him—some, like Leigh, a little too much.

But Blair was taken with him, too.

"I'm afraid of spiders," she shared, wanting to show how much she appreciated his confiding in her. "Even tiny ones give me the willies."

He put his arm along the back of the sofa, making the distance between them seem even smaller. "Guess we'll both be in trouble if we come across a spider sitting on a steep flight of stairs."

Blair laughed. She was really enjoying this talk. She knew how much most men hated admitting even the tiniest weakness, but Josh had confided in her. She found the fact that he felt comfortable with her incredibly appealing. Her gaze dropped to his lips, and she remembered the kiss from this afternoon. Even now, hours later, the thought of his kiss made a tingle of anticipation dance through her.

"Personally, I think you should be afraid of kissing Leigh during rehearsal tomorrow night," Blair said. "She could be hazardous to your health."

"You need to stop worrying about Leigh," he said gently. "By the time the play starts, you'll get the kiss you need."

"That's good."

Feeling him watching her, Blair glanced up. Their gazes locked, and she felt as if she was being pulled down by an undertow. All she could think about was kissing Josh.

And that wasn't smart. A smart woman would say good night before things went too far. A smart woman would recognize danger when she saw it directly in front of her—or rather, next to her on the couch.

So maybe she wasn't very smart after all, because she didn't say good night. She stayed where she was and waited for him to kiss her. Which he didn't—at least not at first. He hesitated, and Blair recognized the indecision crossing his face. He didn't want to be attracted to her any more than she wanted to be attracted to him. But the pull was there, strong and growing stronger with each passing minute.

"I should head over to the apartment," he said softly.

"Probably a good idea," Blair said, even as she was leaning toward him. Her last thought before their lips met was that maybe neither of them was very smart after all.

Josh knew he was only making things worse, but he couldn't help himself. While they had talked, he'd felt closer to Blair than he'd ever felt to another person. Kissing her seemed like the most natural thing in the world.

Besides, what harm could a simple little kiss do? He resolved to keep the kiss light, brief. He could do that. So without thinking anymore, he brushed his lips against hers, savoring the sensation. As her sweet perfume filled his senses, he had an increasingly difficult time remembering his resolution to keep the kiss light. His hands drifted up to cup her cheeks. She was such a sweet, kind woman. She deserved a man who believed in marriage, and who would help her build a life in this small town.

At that thought, he felt his heart ache. He wasn't that man. Slowly, sanity returned. He'd be in deep trouble if he didn't stop things now. He wasn't going to fall in love with Blair, and she needed to know that.

But in reality, he was leading her astray again and he knew it. What was wrong with him? With an anguished groan, he pulled away from her. Leaning his head back, he struggled for control. When she finally met his gaze, he saw confusion and hurt in her expression.

"I shouldn't have done that," he said, brushing his fingers across her cheek.

She looked so beautiful. A flush tinted her cheeks, and even though he knew he'd confused her, she didn't look away.

"I shouldn't have either," she admitted with more honesty than he'd expected.

He stood to put distance between them. He needed to tell her the truth—he owed her that much. "Blair, I'm not the marriage-and-family type. My family specializes in broken hearts. I've seen love fail so many times I no longer believe in ever-lasting love." Holding her gaze, he added, "And I get the feeling you're a firm believer in happily-ever-after. Am I right?"

Her sigh was deep and heartfelt. "Yes. But we only kissed, Josh. I wasn't expecting you to marry me."

"But I don't think either one of us is in the market for a broken heart." He raised one brow, daring her to disagree.

"I guess not."

He held her gaze, needing her to understand. "When this play ends, I'm leaving town."

She brushed her hair away from her face. "Guess we'd better stop kissing each other, then."

"Sounds like the best idea." Which it was. No way was he staying in Raynes longer than necessary. He couldn't.

He used all of his willpower to move away from her. "I'm sorry Blair, but it's better this way."

With a brief good night, he walked out of the house and headed toward Eric's apartment. He'd meant what he'd said to Blair. He didn't want either of them to end up with a broken heart.

Especially not Blair.

Josh was right, Blair decided as she headed down the steps in front of her house the next morning. He was absolutely right—he wasn't the type of man she wanted in her life. She wanted a man who believed in settling down and raising a family, not someone who didn't think marriage could last forever. Deep in her heart, she knew that her marriage would last ... she would *make* it last. Loving someone was possible, and she refused to settle for less.

A little swishing noise caught her attention when she reached her car. Setting her briefcase on the back-seat, she leaned against the car door and looked down the sidewalk. As he'd done the previous day, Josh was tossing newspapers up on the front porches as he went jogging. For a moment she watched him, and he certainly was something to watch. Even from several houses away, she could see how handsome he was.

No wonder she'd gotten carried away last night. Thank goodness they'd come to their senses. Now that they understood each other better, the attraction between them would no doubt fade. At least she hoped it would for her own peace of mind.

Life would be so much simpler if only it came with an instruction manual.

She backed down the driveway and deliberately headed in the opposite direction from where Josh was—no sense looking for trouble. If she fell in love with Josh, she'd end up with a broken heart. He had made it clear last night that he had no intention of staying in Raynes, and she knew he wasn't the type to settle down. After all, he didn't even have a permanent home. And she wasn't blind enough to think that kissing her a couple of times would suddenly turn him into a homebody.

Sure, her white-lace daydreams hadn't exactly worked out so far. And sure, her fiancé admitted he'd never really shared the same dreams with her and jilted her right before their wedding. But she still felt deep inside that the safe road was the one for her—Marshall just hadn't been the right guy. She knew the perfect man was out there somewhere, and if she wanted to find him she had to hold firm to her dreams. Heroes didn't ride up on white horses, and good didn't always triumph over evil, but she still believed in true love.

For that reason she was grateful Josh had stopped them last night. She wasn't up for another broken heart right now. Someday she'd find a man who wanted the same things she did from life—a home and a family in a small town where they could put down roots.

Blair maneuvered her car through the small downtown area of Raynes and parked in front of her office, which was actually an old house that had been restored. Getting out of the car, she waved at some shopowners on her street, then headed inside. Her assistant wouldn't arrive for another ten minutes, so Blair went into the little kitchen and started a pot of coffee.

Someday she'd find that perfect man. But she knew in her heart today wasn't that day . . . and Josh Anderson wasn't that man.

Chapter Five

Josh leaned against the kitchen counter and tucked the phone under his chin while he poured himself a cup of coffee. Even his jog this morning hadn't been able to take his mind off Blair. He'd noticed she'd already left for work by the time he got back from his run . . . which was just as well. He no longer knew what to say to her.

Turning his attention back to the phone, Josh listened as Ed Pattinola, his soon-to-be boss at his upcoming contracting job in L.A., ranted on and on about the latest glitches in their code. Ed was wired this morning and had spent the last five minutes rapidly detailing the almost ridiculous amount of work awaiting Josh.

"We're looking forward to you finally getting here," Ed said when he finished describing all the work to be done. "Our backs are up against the wall on this one."

That statement was followed by another laundry list of all the mini-miracles Josh had to accomplish when he arrived in two weeks. But rather than dreading the upcoming challenge, Josh felt a wave of relief wash through him. Just knowing the job was waiting for him in L.A. made his tension level decline. That job would help him keep his mind on the future . . . and off of Blair.

"Any chance I can convince you to come out now and start early? We sure could use the help, especially with the database." Ed chuckled. "I'm sure I could cough up a little incentive bonus to sweeten the deal."

Josh was tempted. He really was. But he couldn't do that to Blair. He'd promised he'd help her with the play, and he wouldn't break that promise. Plus he hadn't spent much time with Eric yet.

"Sorry. Can't do it," Josh said.

"Are you sure? Even a few extra days would help us a lot. No one here wants to slip the schedules again." There was a long pause, then Ed added, "It seems to me that since we're paying you so much, you could be a little more . . . agreeable."

Josh bit back his retort. As much as he loved his job, he hated it when a manager used his salary against him. And it always seemed to happen. Sooner or later, the manager who'd hired him to clean up a coding mess commented on how much he was paying Josh. Of course, most of them waited until he was actually *working* at the company before they said something. But he wasn't surprised Ed was bringing it up now— his company had one of the worst messes Josh had seen in years. Dates had slipped; commitments had been broken.

Bottom line—they needed him. Which was why he earned top dollar—he was one of the best. He'd worked hard to get where he was, and he wasn't about to feel sorry for charging companies a lot to fix their problems.

"I am being agreeable, Ed. I called to check in." Josh took a sip of his coffee and choked when the too strong brew hit his mouth. He obviously hadn't been paying attention to what he was doing this morning. He'd made coffee strong enough to wake the dead. This coffee fiasco was because he was spending too much time thinking about Blair. Josh poured the coffee into the sink and forced himself to refocus on the phone call.

"I didn't mean anything," Ed finally said, back-peddling fast. "I was just hoping you might be able to break free a little earlier than two weeks."

The quiet despair in the other man's voice made Josh reconsider his hard stand. He knew how large corporations worked. More than likely Ed wasn't even responsible for this mess—he probably didn't even have input into the design of the product. Usually one department decided what would be built and then another department came up with an arbitrary schedule. All of this had probably been dropped in poor Ed's lap with a direct order to make it happen.

No wonder the guy sounded so stressed out. Josh decided to cut him some slack.

"How about I work remotely from here?" Josh offered. "I can get a head start, maybe fix a few of the problems. You can overnight me anything you can't e-mail, and we can set aside some time for a conference call."

"Great idea." The relief was obvious in Ed's voice. "Should work just fine until you get here." Silence stretched between them for a moment, then Ed added, "Thanks, Josh."

"No problem." Grabbing a piece of paper off the kitchen counter, Josh jotted down some notes as Ed gave him an overview of what he would send. Josh would put any long-distance calls on his calling card, just like he had this one. He made a mental note to assure Blair that he wasn't going to leave her or Eric with a five hundred dollar phone bill.

When he and Ed finished, Josh hung up and stood for a moment looking out the apartment window into Blair's back yard. An outrageous phone bill wasn't the only thing he didn't want to leave Blair with—he didn't want to leave her with regrets, either. Even though he knew Blair understood he would leave town as soon as the play finished, he wasn't certain she completely understood there was no way he'd change his mind. *No way.*

For that reason, he was going to try his hardest to make certain he didn't lead her astray again. After all, there was only so much guilt a man could carry around with him.

"Tell me every juicy detail," Theresa said, leaning across the table toward Blair.

They were having lunch at the small diner across the street from her office, and Blair was already sorry she'd agreed to come. Theresa was hungry for gossip, but Blair had no intention of feeding her any.

"There aren't any juicy details to tell you. Josh and I went to Burgerland for dinner, then went home. I saw him out jogging this morning, but I didn't talk to him. And you'll see him tonight at rehearsal, the same as I will." Hoping she'd ended this inquisition, Blair picked up her menu and pretended to study the choices.

But Theresa wasn't fooled. "Drop the act. You always order the same thing, so I know you're just hiding."

Sighing, Blair folded up the menu and tucked it behind the ketchup and mustard. "I was hiding because I don't have anything to tell you. Zip. Zero. Zilch." As much as she hated lying to her friend, Blair felt strongly that what happened with Josh was their own business and no one else's.

Theresa tipped her head and studied Blair. "Why don't I believe you?" Her eyes sparkled with devilment. "I know why—because you're too jumpy and jittery for something not to have happened. You're the world's worst liar, and you know it."

"I'm not lying to you. Nothing important happened," Blair said.

"Fine. Don't tell me," Theresa said with a hint of martyrdom. "All I know is, one look from Josh Anderson could melt ice during a snow storm. His picture is in the dictionary next to the word 'gorgeous.' So if you want to pretend that you're not attracted to him, that's fine with me. I'll sit over here and pretend I'm still a size six and men drool over me."

Blair laughed, and her tension evaporated. "Lots of men find you attractive."

Theresa chuckled. "Old, blind men. And my husband, but that's because he still sees me the way I was the day we met, when I kissed him in my dad's office."

Despite herself, Blair couldn't resist asking, "You kissed Carl the first day you met him?"

Theresa made a big show of arranging her napkin

in her lap. "I thought you didn't want to discuss the men in our lives."

Blair leaned back in the seat. "Josh isn't the man in my life, and forget I asked about Carl."

Looking up, Theresa said, "Carl was a summer hire at my father's law firm, and I was home visiting from college. The second I met him, I knew he was the one for me. So I kissed him to show him how I felt." Theresa arched one brow and took a well-timed sip of her iced tea. When she set the glass back on the table, she said, "Poor thing, I really surprised him. But at least he understood how I felt about him."

Stunned, Blair just stared at her. "I can't believe you did that. What if your father had walked in?"

"Oh, he did. But thankfully, he liked Carl, so Dad didn't get mad."

With a laugh, Blair said, "Well, you're braver than I am."

"No, I'm not brave. I just knew in my heart he was the one. So I acted on that feeling." With a wink at Blair, she added, "Nothing's to be gained by standing on the sidelines in life. You've got to jump right into the game."

"I'm not standing on the sidelines." Blair said. "Josh isn't the right man for me. He isn't interested in settling down and starting a family."

Theresa smiled a Cheshire-cat smile. "Okay, if you say so."

"I say so," Blair said firmly, returning her attention to her menu. "And I mean it."

Thankfully the waitress showed up, forcing them to change the subject. The young woman wrote down their order and then scurried off.

Once they were alone again, Theresa said, "Well, if Josh isn't the right man for you, then you need to keep looking. Nothing like being in love to make a woman cheerful. And I am *one* cheerful woman."

Despite herself, Blair laughed. Theresa was indeed the most cheerful woman she'd ever met, and the more the older woman sat grinning at her, the more Blair laughed.

"You are a happy lady," Blair admitted.

Theresa continued to grin. "You betcha. And it's because I adore my husband." The smile on Theresa's face faltered, then faded. "You know, I don't want you to get hurt, Blair, but I will tell you one thing. When I met Carl, he wasn't planning on staying in town, either. He was just here for the summer, then he was going on to Shreveport. I changed his mind."

Theresa couldn't seriously be suggesting what she seemed to be. "You expect me to try to change Josh's mind about leaving?"

"Oh, no. Not at all. I'm just saying that Carl thought he didn't want to settle down either, but look how happy the two of us are. Once we fell in love, Carl didn't leave because he wanted to stay with me."

"That's wonderful for you, Theresa, but it won't work that way for me. Josh isn't Carl. He isn't a college kid just starting out. He has a career and he knows what he wants—and doesn't want—from life. I want a husband who loves living in Raynes as much as I do."

Theresa nodded. "I understand how you feel. I really do. But Blair, just because a fish is different doesn't mean it can't learn to swim in your pond."

Blair blinked. "What?"

"You know what I mean. Don't write Josh off just because he seems to have different plans. And don't assume that everything you think you want out of life is the only thing that will make you happy." Theresa leaned forward, her grin almost too big for her face. "Just remember, honey, I'm an extremely happy woman, and my cheery outlook has nothing to do with living in Raynes, Texas. It's solely based on being crazy in love with my husband."

There was a pretty nurse in Eric's room when Josh arrived, just like yesterday. As had become his habit, Josh waited patiently in the doorway while the woman fussed and fidgeted over Eric. After she left, Josh came in and sat in the chair next to the bed. Stretching his legs out in front of him, he cocked his head and gave Eric a pointed look.

"What?" Eric laughed at his own attempt to pretend

innocence. "Hey, it's a friendly hospital. What can I say?"

Josh couldn't help but smile. "Man, when you're dead, you're going to be flirting with the woman in the next grave."

"If she's single."

With a chuckle, Josh settled back in the plastic chair. Even in the couple of days Josh had been around, he'd noticed a remarkable improvement in Eric's condition. At this rate, it wouldn't be long before Eric got out of here.

Josh nodded toward the casts his friend wore. "It's amazing what some guys will do to get a pretty nurse to notice them."

Eric grinned. "Take a hike. So, how's the play going?"

Josh shrugged. "Fine. No problems."

That much was true. The play wasn't causing him any problems—just Blair was. Or, rather, being in close proximity to Blair was. But he could hardly tell Eric he was having a hard time resisting his sister.

Josh stood and wandered over to the window, looking at the assortment of get well cards displayed on the sill. Not surprisingly, most of them were from women.

"Bob Julian stopped by," Eric said, his voice tinted with laughter. "He told me he was doing a fantastic job playing the part of the King, but that you had some trouble with Leigh last night."

As much as Josh liked the older man, he couldn't help wishing Bob had kept his mouth shut. At this rate, the entire town would know by the end of the day. Leaning back against the windowsill, Josh looked at Eric. "Bob's mistaken. Everything's fine."

"That's not what I heard," Eric said. "Bob's exact words were that 'Leigh kissed you hard enough for your ancestors to feel it.' "

"Doesn't anyone in this town have anything better to talk about?" The feeling of being watched bothered Josh. In a small town, everyone knew everything. He'd grown up knowing the whole town disapproved of the way his parents lived their lives. He'd heard the gossip. Small towns made him feel claustrophobic.

"Bob's exaggerating," Josh said, hoping to move off the subject.

Although Eric's face still showed bruises and cuts from the accident, nothing dimmed his million-watt grin. "I don't think so. From what I hear, the turnout for the play should break local records. Everyone's going to come to see what happens between you and Leigh. Think I'll ask one of these nice nurses to go and tape the show so I can watch it."

Josh was about to set Eric straight about a few things, but before he could say anything Blair walked in. When she saw him, her steps faltered.

She looked from Eric to Josh then back to her brother. "Sorry. I didn't expect you to have company."

Eric shot her a confused look. "I don't have company. It's only Josh." He nodded toward the other chair in the small room. "Sit. This is a real treat. Normally, no one stops by in the middle of the day to see me."

Blair rolled her eyes at his mock-pathetic tone. Smiling, she glanced at Josh, but her gaze quickly skittered away. "Oh, please. Sell that to someone who's buying. I bet you had at least one nurse in here doting attention on you when Josh arrived."

"She was a blond." Josh stood and walked over to the door, putting some distance between himself and Blair. Being close to her short-circuited his common sense. But even from across the room, he felt the pull between them. He found himself watching her. As much as he hated admitting it, he'd missed her this morning. She'd left her house before he'd gotten back from his run—probably on purpose.

Studying her now, he was struck again by how pretty she was. Today she had on a conservative pale blue suit. She'd pulled her hair back in a ponytail, held in place by a large navy blue bow. Personally, he preferred her in casual clothes, like those she'd had on last night.

But how Blair dressed was none of his concern. Josh glanced at Eric, who sat watching both of them intently. Josh should have guessed his friend would get suspicious. The tension level in the room had shot through the roof since Blair arrived. Someone as astute as Eric wouldn't miss what was happening here.

"I think I'll shove off," Josh said. His gaze met Blair's, and this time, she didn't look away. Instead, she frowned slightly. He'd give anything to know what she was thinking. Was she angry with him? More importantly, did she regret kissing him last night?

"You don't have to leave just because I stopped by," she said, still looking at him.

No. He had to leave before he drove himself crazy. "I have some things I need to do. Besides, I'm sure you and Eric would like to visit."

Eric snorted. "We don't have any secrets to discuss." He looked at his sister. "So what brings you over so early in the day? Bet it wasn't me."

Blair looked flustered. She glanced away from Josh and turned her attention to her brother. A full thirty seconds ticked by before she said, "You're right. I came to see Donna Mason's baby. Since I was here, I thought I'd see you, too."

"What's the baby look like?" Eric asked.

"I haven't stopped by the nursery yet."

"Ha." Eric grinned at his sister. "I knew you couldn't resist seeing me first. Just as well, once you get to the nursery, it will take hours for the nurses to pry you away from there."

Eric's comment shot a sharp pain through Josh's chest. *Babies. Wouldn't it figure that Blair loved babies?* If he'd had any doubts they weren't meant to be together, this cinched it. He'd been right from the beginning: Blair wanted a family.

"I really do have to go." Josh headed halfway out the door, promising to visit Eric the next day. Then he glanced back at Blair. "Guess I'll see you this evening."

She nodded. "Sure."

For a second, he just looked at her. Then he walked out.

No two ways around it—he needed to leave this town—and soon.

Blair caught up with Josh by the elevators. "Eric just made a good suggestion. Want to see where the money from the play is going to be spent?"

She knew it was a lame excuse her brother had given her just so she could talk to Josh, but she appreciated it nonetheless. She needed to do something to defuse the tension level between them before tonight when they had to face the rest of the cast.

For a moment, she watched indecision cross Josh's face. It didn't take a genius to see that he wanted to escape right now, but when the elevator doors opened, he nodded.

"Sure." He followed her into the elevator. "What floor?"

"Three." After the door slid silently shut, Blair sucked in a deep breath and blurted, "I hope you're not upset about last night."

Josh turned and looked at her. "Upset? No, I'm not upset. How about you?"

"No." She wove her fingers together. This wasn't easy. "And I think we came to the right decision. About not kissing anymore."

"Yeah."

She shot a quick glance at the elevator panel. They were almost to the third floor, and she wanted to get this settled. "I hope we can try to be friends . . . for Eric's sake."

Josh's expression was impossible to read. "We can try."

Before he could add anything else, the doors opened and they walked into what was obviously the play-room for the children's ward. The small amount of toys scattered around a few worn plastic tables was pitiful. Since the hospital was the only one around for almost a hundred miles, it served a lot of people. Many of those people had no insurance, so whenever the question of buying more toys came up, there just wasn't any money in the budget. But Blair had to give Leigh credit—she'd found a way to raise money for more toys.

In the far corner of the room was a lopsided easel. A boy of about eight or nine sat in front of it, slightly hunched over in his chair and drawing with earnest concentration.

Blair watched in fascination as Josh wandered around the room, stopping now and then to straighten a puzzle or pick up a toy. When he neared the far end of the room, the boy turned and looked at him. A large bandage covered one side of the child's face and part of his head. Clearly whatever had happened to the boy had been very serious. Blair felt her chest tighten—she couldn't stand to see a child hurt.

But Josh didn't even flinch. Instead, he simply nodded toward the easel. "That's a pretty good drawing of a '57 Chevy. You must like cars."

The kid nodded solemnly. "Someday I'm going to buy myself one of these cars and fix it up. Then I'll drive it real far and real fast."

Away from here.

Blair heard the boy's silent words and she knew Josh heard them, too. The sight of the tall, strong man and the injured boy got to Blair. She stared down at her shoes, willing herself not to cry.

When she looked back up, Josh was crouched next to the boy, giving him some tips on the finer details of the car. They were still in deep conversation several minutes later when a nurse appeared in the doorway.

"Danny, it's time to go back to your room." She gave Blair a small smile. "He's our resident wanderer. Every time we turn around, he's gone."

Danny stood slowly, and Blair realized the boy was covering up the pain he felt. Josh stood, too, and shook the boy's hand.

"Nice to meet a fellow motorhead," Josh said.

Danny's face split in a wide grin. "Yeah. Nice to meet you, too."

At that moment Blair realized she was coming dangerously close to falling hard for Josh Anderson.

Chapter Six

"Could be worse, I suppose," Theresa said with forced cheerfulness as she came to stand next to Blair. "At least Evie's a warm body."

Blair smiled lamely. Tonight was the dress rehearsal, and nothing was going right. One of the stepsisters had developed laryngitis, and although the make-up artist had volunteered to take her place, Evie was struggling with the lines.

"Yes, she is a warm body." Blair scanned her copy of the script. Evie's character had over fifty lines in the play. It was a lot of dialogue to ask the woman to learn overnight.

But Evie kept assuring everyone she could learn the lines, and at this point, Blair had no choice but to trust her. Glancing at her watch, she decided to start. Everyone had arrived but Josh, who no doubt would show up eventually. His character didn't come on stage until the middle of the play, so they didn't have to wait for him.

Blair had been hoping Josh might arrive before the rest of the cast so they could talk some more. They hadn't had much of a chance at the hospital. After they left the children's ward, she went on alone to the nursery to see the baby.

Well, there was no sense waiting any longer for Josh.

Blair asked the actors to take their positions and they started rehearsal. Within minutes, the door at the back of the auditorium opened. Blair didn't have to turn around to know the new arrival was Josh. She could sense him, almost as if they were attuned to each other. Her sensation was foolish, but she couldn't shake it. When he reached the stage, he gave her an apologetic smile and then headed backstage to change into his costume.

Blair forced herself not to think about the man who already took up far too much of her concentration. She had the actors find their places again, and they resumed.

Slowly, they progressed through the play, stopping occasionally to smooth out a rough spot. Everyone looked so wonderful in their costumes that the audience would no doubt overlook minor errors. In fact, once the ball began and the women appeared in their long, sparkling gowns, Blair could almost imagine the look of enchantment that would surely cover the children's faces.

When Josh came on stage, Blair had to keep a tight grip on her clipboard. He looked . . . spectacular. The deep blue suit, with its high collar and myriad of ribbons and medals, made him look like someone who had truly stepped out of a child's imagination. Blair was certain that when she'd been five, Josh epitomized her idea of Prince Charming. In many ways, he epitomized that man now. Today in the hospital had shown her once more how kind he was.

Leigh appeared at the back of the stage. She, too, looked wonderful. Her shimmery white gown, coupled with her pale blond hair, transformed her into a vision. When Josh took Leigh in his arms and they started to dance, Blair noted that everyone on stage stood transfixed. Nothing like the sight of two extraordinarily beautiful people together to make a mere mortal stop and stare.

After the dance ended, Josh and Leigh said their lines without any errors, although Leigh once again stood far too close to her co-star. Blair mentioned it briefly, and then let them continue. When it was time for the kiss, Blair was filled with dread. Josh bent his head, his lips brushing Leigh's in an obviously chaste kiss. As much as she hated to admit it, the sight of Josh kissing another woman made her more than a little jealous. Which was ridiculous—Josh was only kissing Leigh because of the play. Besides, she didn't want to get involved with the man. She had absolutely no right to feel jealous.

Unfortunately, though, she did. When the kiss ended without incident, Blair released the breath she hadn't realized she'd been holding. As Josh began to lift his head, Leigh suddenly snaked her arms around his neck and tried to pull him back for another kiss.

"Leigh," Blair said, the anger in her tone more than enough warning. Josh moved Leigh away from him, and she slowly dropped her arms from around his neck. He shot his co-star a warning look, but continued with the play.

From that moment on, the play seemed to take forever to end. Everyone kept looking at Josh, expecting him to get angry. But he seemed to take Leigh's overture in stride. Blair, however, felt her blood pressure rising. Leigh was deliberately baiting Josh, which could have serious complications. What if Josh decided to quit the play? No way could they find a replacement at this late date.

When rehearsal finally ended, Blair congratulated everyone, then headed across the stage toward Leigh, wanting to head her off before she escaped to the makeshift dressing rooms.

"Leigh, I thought you understood how important it is to keep the kiss circumspect," Blair said firmly.

Leigh didn't appear even a little embarrassed. She merely shrugged. "I promise I'll behave tomorrow night."

"You've said that before. Leigh, you can't keep doing this." Blair struggled to keep her voice from rising. "You're not being fair to Josh."

Josh stepped forward, laying his hand on Blair's arm. "I'm sure Leigh knows better than to try something like that during a real performance."

Blair felt her stomach knot as Leigh smiled at Josh. "Is that true?" Blair asked the older woman. "Can we trust you tomorrow?"

"Blair, you're much too serious. I was only kidding." There was just enough bite in Leigh's voice that Blair knew she was not at all pleased at being called on her behavior. Coldness settled around Leigh like a shawl.

"Well, I don't find it funny." Blair struggled to gain control of her temper. She didn't want to blow this out of proportion, and she was honest enough with herself to know she might be overreacting somewhat because of her confused feelings for Josh. But regardless of how she felt, Leigh was wrong. "You can't kiss him like that again," Blair finally said.

"I *can't*?" Leigh laughed. "This is my play. You're making a big deal out of nothing. If you understood men at all, you'd know that Josh isn't upset by a measly little kiss." She met Blair's gaze. "Then again, if you understood men, maybe you wouldn't have lost your fiancé."

Blair had kept her voice down so the others wouldn't hear their discussion, but Leigh had no such restraint. Her words were loud enough to reach the rest of the cast. Blair felt like she'd been bushwhacked. She could feel the group watching her, waiting for her reaction. Until this moment, Blair hadn't realized that Leigh knew about her past. And if Leigh knew, then undoubtedly a lot of people in town knew.

Marshall's defection had hurt, but that pain was in the past. Blair knew that she had nothing to be ashamed of. Still, she couldn't help feeling embarrassed that everyone in town knew she'd been jilted.

The silence in the auditorium was absolute. Finally, Josh moved toward her. "Blair—"

She waved aside his sympathy. If she wanted to face herself in the morning, she had to handle this confrontation with Leigh herself. Stoking up her will, Blair forced herself to face the older woman.

"My relationship with my ex-fiancé has nothing to do with the play, Leigh. I need your assurance that you won't kiss Josh like that tomorrow. *You* were the one who asked me to help with the play. To do that, I need your promise."

Leigh had the decency to look a bit ashamed for her

remark. "I already promised, and I mean it. No more kidding around."

"Thank you." Blair forced a smile to cross her lips. "Now let's get everyone out of their costumes and call it a night."

Almost at once, the actors and crew started talking again. A few shot quick glances her way, but no one approached her. No one except Josh. When everyone had moved off to the dressing rooms, he placed his hand on her arm.

"Are you okay?"

"I'm fine." She bent to pick up her clipboard. "Why don't you go change? I'm sure you'd like to get out of that costume."

Josh studied her closely, and Blair forced herself not to look away. "I can go talk to Leigh," he offered.

Blair shook her head. "She gave me her promise, and I believe she'll keep it."

"I wasn't talking about the kiss. I meant I can talk to her about what she said . . . about you. It was a low blow."

He said the last few words with enough force that Blair realized he was angry—on *her* behalf. How interesting. Or rather, it would be interesting if she cared how he felt about her. But she didn't. Not one little bit. She wasn't going to get involved with Josh. Okay, it was difficult to remember all the reasons why she should avoid him when he stood there looking at her with kindness and more than a hint of attraction in his gorgeous eyes. But she had to resist.

Off in the distance, Blair could hear the other members of the cast talking and laughing. The sounds brought her back to her senses. She cleared her throat. "Thanks for the offer, but there's no reason for you to talk to Leigh. I'm fine."

Josh didn't look convinced, but thankfully, he let the matter drop. "Would you like to grab something to eat after I change my clothes?"

She wished she could, because they could talk during dinner. But life seemed to be against her tonight. "I can't. I have to finish some work for a new client. But there should be plenty of food in my refrigerator if Eric doesn't have any. Help yourself."

He gave her a considered look. "You're sure you're okay?"

"Yes." Glancing at the clipboard in her hands, Blair wasn't surprised to see she was clutching it so tightly her knuckles were almost white. With effort, she relaxed.

Josh patted her shoulder. "Then I'll see you back at the house later."

Tingles danced down Blair's arm at the light contact. Long after he'd disappeared backstage, she stood looking after him. *Why'd he have to be so nice?* Resisting him was difficult enough without him being a terrific guy on top of being so handsome.

What she needed now was a healthy dose of will-power, because she had the sinking feeling hers was starting to run out.

He was playing with fire, Josh decided as he entered Blair's house an hour later. No matter how much he wanted to convince himself he could have a friendship with Blair and nothing else, he was afraid he couldn't. He was just too attached to her not to think about the possibility of something more.

Tonight, he'd been furious at Leigh for embarrassing Blair. His feelings had been more than simply those of a friend; he wanted to protect her, to make up for Leigh's spitefulness.

Which meant he was in serious trouble. He cared about Blair. Oh, sure, he was too smart to fall in love. But even caring about her was bad, especially if Blair came to realize how he felt.

With a groan of self-disgust, he headed toward the kitchen. He wanted to make dinner so Blair could eat as soon as she got home from work. Unloading the groceries, Josh quickly put everything away except what he needed to make the spaghetti sauce. Although he was hardly a gourmet cook, he could make a few simple dishes.

After the sauce was cooking gently on the stove, he wiped off the counters. As he worked, he noticed the faucet in the sink dripped. He crossed back over to make certain he'd turned it off. He had. That drip would have to be taken care of . . . soon.

With a sigh, he admitted defeat. He could never let the faucet drip all night, wasting water like that. Without stopping to consider the wisdom of his of his actions, he opened the cabinet under the sink. Sure enough, Blair kept her toolbox there, just like Eric had in his last apartment. Looking through it, Josh found what he needed and set to work.

Once the sink was fixed, Josh returned the tools to the toolbox. While he was cleaning up, the doorbell rang. Expecting it to be one of Blair's neighbors, he opened the door—and tensed when he saw it was Leigh. Just what he needed—a visit from the spider woman.

Her smile was tentative. "Mind if I come in?"

Josh leaned against the doorjamb. Since Blair wasn't home, he didn't feel it was his place to invite Leigh into the house. Not to mention the fact that he he didn't *want* to invite her in. "What's up?"

The chill in his voice wasn't lost on Leigh. Her smile faded. "I just stopped by to apologize to Blair. I shouldn't have been so . . ."

"Mean?"

Leigh narrowed her eyes. "Thoughtless." She craned her head, trying to see around him. "Is Blair home? I didn't get a chance to talk to her after rehearsal."

"She's not here." He could tell Leigh expected him to tell her where Blair was, but Josh didn't share that information. In his opinion, the people in this town knew *way* too much about each other as it was.

Leigh took a step forward. "You don't like me, do you?"

"You haven't done much for me to like." He knew giving Leigh the unvarnished truth wouldn't win him any popularity points, but he didn't care. As far as he was concerned, Leigh needed a good dose of reality.

She drummed her long nails against her purse while she considered him. Oddly enough, she didn't appear offended by his statement. "Most people do like me."

"Like you or your money?"

With a very unladylike snort, she said, "You may have a point there. But I'm not the witch you think I am."

Josh ran a tired hand across his jaw. "Look, Leigh, it doesn't matter to me what you are. I'm only here for a few days. But I think you should consider how your actions affect the people around you. This is a small town, and it wouldn't be too difficult for these people to turn against you."

His candor seemed to surprise her. "Maybe that's where my money comes in handy."

"When push comes to shove, your money isn't going to buy you anything that really matters. I would think a bright lady like you would have figured that out by now."

She laughed, but the sound lacked any sincerity. "Thanks for the twelve second analysis."

Josh shrugged, levering away from the doorframe. "Take it or leave it. I'm only telling you what I see."

"Regardless of what you think of me, I stopped by tonight to apologize to Blair. I shouldn't have brought up her fiancé, and I really am sorry."

Scanning her face, he realized she was sincere. Leigh did seem to be sorry. "I'll tell Blair you stopped by."

Leigh moved forward, placing her hand lightly on his arm. "Also tell her what I said. Tell her I'm sorry. Blair's a nice woman, and I didn't mean to hurt her."

Josh wasn't surprised Leigh felt badly. Blair was a nice woman, one who didn't deserve to be ridiculed.

"I'll tell her, but you should, too. Tomorrow night you should repeat your apology."

"Fine." Leigh sighed loudly. "Tell me, are you always such an ogre?"

Josh smiled. "Yes, ma'am, I am."

"Then I'm incredibly glad you didn't fall in love with me. I've never cared for men who don't find me enchanting."

He couldn't help laughing. "I can understand why."

With a little wave, Leigh headed for the front steps. When she reached them, she turned to look back at him. "Let me be an example to you, Josh Anderson. Blair doesn't deserve to be hurt . . . by either one of us."

With that as her parting shot, Leigh walked away. Long after she'd pulled out of the driveway, Josh stood in the doorway, looking out into the night. He knew Leigh was right—Blair didn't deserve to be hurt. By either one of them.

Blair found Josh on the back porch, repairing the broken railing. For a moment, she just watched, appreciating the view. Even objectively, he was an incredibly good-looking man. No wonder Leigh kept throwing herself at him.

"Isn't it too dark to work out here?" she finally asked.

He didn't appear startled that she was home, so he'd probably known she was standing in the doorway, gawking at him. *Great.* She could add that to the other embarrassments of tonight.

Josh stopped hammering and glanced at her over his shoulder. "The overhead lights are enough to work by. Let me just secure a few more boards, and I'll be done. Then I'll finish up dinner."

"You don't have to fix my house and cook for me," she said, picking up a hammer and coming over to help. "You're a guest here."

Even over the loud pounding noise of his hammer,

Blair could hear him laugh. "A guest you didn't invite."

He was right, of course, but she'd be lying if she said she didn't like having him around. She liked having him here a lot. Too much. Absently, she put part of the railing in place and drove a nail through the wood.

Josh looked at her again, his blue eyes appearing dark in the overhead light. Beyond them, the backyard was cloaked in blackness.

"Did you get all your work done?" he asked.

"Yes. Sorry to abandon you." She studied the board she'd just nailed in place. It didn't look quite right.

"You didn't abandon me." He finished hammering, then walked over to stand next to her. "Leigh stopped by a little while ago to apologize."

Blair forgot about the board and looked at him. "I bet she *really* stopped by to see you."

Josh shook his head. "I don't think so. I think she feels badly about what she did." He studied her intently for several breathless moments. "Leigh knows you didn't deserve her attack."

His gaze sent Blair's heart into an erratic rhythm. She tried to calm down, focusing instead on what he'd told her. Although she guessed that Leigh regretted her hastily spoken words, Blair hadn't expected her to be bothered by the incident for more than a few minutes.

"I'll call Leigh in the morning and tell her not to

worry." While alone at the office, Blair thought about what had happened. It really wasn't a big deal if the town knew about her broken engagement . . . not really.

Blair became uncomfortable as Josh continued to study her. She was pretty certain she knew what he wanted to talk about, so she decided to make things easy for both of them. She glanced at the hammer in her hand, not wanting to look at him while she told him the story.

"His name was Marshall Ross. We were engaged for six months. A couple of weeks before the wedding, he was offered a job that would have required us to move every year or so. When I told him I couldn't stand the thought of living like a nomad again, he initially said he wouldn't take the job—it wasn't even a promotion. But the day before the wedding, he told me he'd changed his mind. He didn't want to settle down, and he'd decided to take the job. Then he left."

When Josh laid his hand over hers, she felt a tightness in her throat. Surprisingly, she wasn't upset about Marshall. It was Josh's tenderness that got to her.

"Actually, I'm glad we broke up," she said. "Marshall was right. We weren't meant to be together."

Hazarding a glance at Josh, she found him watching her closely. "You don't have to tell me this," he said.

"I wanted to explain, and it no longer bothers me to talk about it. We were too different and should have figured it out sooner." She shrugged, trying to be non-chalant. "Maybe Leigh is right . . . maybe I don't understand men."

Josh leaned forward. "Of course she isn't right."

He seemed so convinced. So certain. But when it came right down to it, Josh didn't know very much about her. She hadn't planned on confiding in him this way, but the tenderness in his eyes was her undoing. Thinking back, she remembered the kindness he'd shown the boy in the hospital. How was she supposed to resist him if he kept being so wonderful?

"Well, it's water under the bridge now," she said.

"But it's why you moved to Raynes, isn't it?"

She tucked a stray strand of hair behind one ear. "In a way, I guess. But now I feel like I belong here."

He smiled at her gently, and her pulse kicked into a frantic beat. "So rather than being part of a couple, you've decided to be part of a town, right?"

Deep down, Blair knew she should drop the subject. They were wading into deep and dangerous waters. But she couldn't back away, and she couldn't break the spell settling around them. Instead, she focused on his touch and the kindness in his eyes. She felt as if she'd been alone all her life.

"Something like that." With a little laugh, she added, "I guess everyone likes to believe they're special."

Josh moved closer until he brushed against her lightly. "You are special, Blair."

Standing this close, she could feel his warmth, and the temptation to touch him was incredibly strong.

"Look at all the great things you do for the people around you." His voice had a husky timbre that snared Blair in an emotional web. Gazing deep into his eyes, she saw conflict. Like her, he knew they should be fighting against this attraction. But like her, Josh seemed to be at a loss as to how to combat chemistry this potent. It was like trying to extinguish an inferno with an eyedropper.

"Thank you for saying that." She looked at his lips, longing for him to kiss her. Whether it was a wise decision or not, she wanted him to hold her in his arms again. She wanted to feel his lips against her own.

By slow degrees, he slid one arm around her waist, pulling her close. "This is probably a mistake."

"Definitely." The word came out as a breathless whisper. "But I don't care."

Josh bent his head and placed his lips against hers. "Neither do I," he murmured. Then he kissed her.

Chapter Seven

If anything, her lips were softer, sweeter than the last time they'd kissed. All of the excellent reasons he had not to kiss Blair shuttled to the back of Josh's mind. Blair felt wonderful in his arms. Her response was warm, open—more than he probably deserved but less than he wanted. Even though he knew kissing her was selfish, he was reluctant to end the embrace.

Still, common sense eventually grabbed hold of him, and he released her.

He ran one hand through his hair. "I guess I need to apologize yet again. I'm getting a lot of practice apologizing."

Blair smiled slightly and moved away from him. "Me, too."

Sighing, Josh packed up the tools he'd been using. When he turned to face her, he said, "Blair, I'm not interested in settling down, in getting married." He drew a ragged breath into his lungs. "I can't offer you anything, but I don't seem to be able to resist you."

"I seem to be having that problem, too. But don't worry about a few kisses, Josh. I know you don't intend on staying in Raynes. I don't expect you to."

Josh studied her. Blair was letting him off the hook, and he knew it. She was a sweet lady who deserved much better than he could offer. She deserved the fairy tale, the happy home, the laughing children.

Prince Charming.

"Are you still interested in dinner?" he asked, holding the back door to the house open for her.

As she passed him, she gave him a small smile. There and then, Josh made a vow to himself. He only had a few more days in town. Surely he could find the strength to resist Blair for that long. If not for his sake, than for hers.

"I read in a magazine article that being in love gives your complexion a glow." Theresa flashed Blair a smug grin as she fiddled with her costume. "Your skin has a real glow today."

Blair glanced at the older woman. There was absolutely no way Theresa could know what she was thinking . . . how she was feeling . . . how much Josh had come to mean to her. Which meant Theresa's guess was just that—a guess. And if she didn't get flustered, the other woman would remain none the wiser.

"My skin looks the same as always." Blair finished tacking a piece of loose ribbon to Theresa's costume and backed up a few steps to survey the result. Although officially the director, Blair's real job was chief problem-solver. Anything broken, she fixed. They were opening in ten minutes, and as far as Blair could tell, *everything* was broken. For the past two hours, she'd run from cast member to cast member, repairing costumes, helping with makeup, and soothing nerves. If she survived tonight, she might make it through the entire run of the play.

"Blair, you can pretend you're not a happy woman, but I know better. You, my friend, are indeed glowing. I think it's love."

"I'm sweating because I'm nervous, not because I'm in love." Blair rolled her eyes and walked off. Now wasn't the time to have this conversation with Theresa. Truthfully, she didn't know what to call her feelings for Josh. She cared for him. Deeply. But she wasn't ready to call those feelings love.

Looking for something else to focus on, she headed off to make one more pass through the cast members, making sure that everyone was ready. For opening night, they all seemed to be in high spirits. As far as she could tell, she was the only one suffering from jitters.

When Josh came out of the men's dressing room, he looked impossibly handsome in his blue suit. Blair's pulse did its familiar flutter. Maybe her jitters weren't due to nerves after all. She hadn't seen him since dinner last night, and he'd been out jogging when she woke up. Being more than a little cowardly, she'd once again left for work without waiting for him to get back to the house.

Josh stopped when he saw her, his direct gaze intense across the distance separating them. "Hi," he said.

"Hi," she managed back, her voice husky.

He flashed her a smile that made her heart do a little limbo dance. "Did you have a good day?"

"Yes. You?"

"Eric was in a grumpy mood, but yeah, for the most part it was a good day. See you later."

With that, he walked away to join the rest of the cast. Blair counted to ten, willing her heart to slow its beat to something approaching normal. She wasn't completely successful, but when she finally felt some semblance of calm, she approached the cast. After telling them to break a leg, she headed to her post, praying silently for good luck. Every seat in the auditorium was filled, so if the play bombed, it looked like they'd do it in front of a fair percentage of the town's population.

The night had turned out well, Josh decided after he'd changed backstage and joined the rest of the cast. Everything, or at least almost everything, had gone as planned, including the kiss. For once, Leigh had behaved.

Josh scanned the backstage area looking for Blair. He finally spotted her on the other side, talking to some people from town. She was the local hero tonight. The performance had been a huge hit, and from what he heard, tickets for the remaining nights had almost sold out.

When Blair noticed him, she headed his direction, bringing a group of young children with her. Blair looked so natural surrounded by children that a tightness wrapped around Josh's heart, but he ignored the emotions clamoring through him.

"Josh, I'd like you to meet some friends of mine." Blair quickly introduced him to the children, explaining that he played Prince Charming. A few of the little girls looked at him like he'd hung the moon, so he knelt down to smile at them. He expected them to be shy, but instead, they immediately swarmed him.

"So, are you *really* Prince Charming?" a blond girl asked, tipping her head and studying him closely.

"Of course he's not. Not really. He's just playing

him. You know, dress up." The oldest member of the group, a tall girl with dark hair and serious eyes handed out this information. "See, he doesn't have his prince clothes on anymore."

The blond frowned, considering what her friend said. "Maybe he really is Prince Charming. He could have changed so he won't get his prince clothes dirty. My mom won't let me play in my school clothes when I get home." She gave Josh a pensive look. "Are you really a prince?"

Josh held back his amusement. As much as he hated destroying their illusions, he had to set them straight. Hoping to soften the blow, he smiled and said gently, "I'm afraid I'm not really a prince."

"See. I told you." The dark haired girl folded her arms across her thin chest. "He doesn't have any prince clothes or medals or nothing. He's just a regular boy."

He could see a smile tugging at Blair's lips. It turned into a full grin when one of the girls in the group decided he had serious cooties. With a squeal, the group ran across the stage to talk to Leigh instead. The small blond trailed behind, still looking at Josh.

"Guess I'm not the draw that Cinderella is," Josh said as he rose to his feet.

Blair laughed. "Too bad about the cooties thing."

Her eyes twinkled with humor, and he couldn't re-member ever wanting to kiss a woman as much as he did right now. Involuntarily, he leaned toward Blair, stopping when he heard the children chattering in the distance.

"I've gotten used to them," he said.

Blair chuckled softly. "That's good. Hey, if you're not busy, the cast and crew are going out to celebrate our success. Want to come along?"

Josh agreed, but as they left the auditorium, he knew the reason he'd said yes had nothing to do with the celebration and everything to do with wanting to be with Blair.

Oh, boy, was he ever in trouble.

"Leigh seems to have found a live one," Bob Julian said loudly enough to be heard over the deafening rock music being belted out by a small band.

Blair glanced out on the tiny dance floor. Leigh was dancing with an attractive older man. If memory served her, this was Leigh's third or fourth dance partner in the last few minutes. But this man looked like he would challenge all others. Ignoring the fast tempo of the music, he held Leigh closely as they slow danced.

Bob winked at his wife. "Looks like Leigh's finally found someone else to bother rather than Josh."

The cast laughed, and Blair felt her gaze naturally land on Josh. He smiled at her, and she felt the zing of attraction shoot through her. Of course, she felt a lot more than simple attraction for him. Watching him with the children tonight had made her admit to herself once again that she was falling for him.

But more than likely, Josh's feelings for her didn't run any deeper than simple male-female chemistry. Still, at least he was honest with her, something Marshall had never been.

When the music turned soft and slow, Josh stood and came to stand next to Blair's chair. He extended his hand, and wordlessly, she took it. On the dance floor, she slipped into his arms, feeling as if she'd come home.

For a few timeless moments, they swayed to the music. Blair allowed herself the luxury of holding him closely, pretending for this short time that he really was hers. That they had a future together.

But her dreams were just that—dreams. Blair forced herself not to dwell on what she couldn't have. Instead, she focused on what she had now—Josh, holding her tightly in his arms.

"You were wonderful tonight," she murmured.

He chuckled deep in his chest. "I didn't do anything except stand around and look royal."

"Well, you made the perfect Prince Charming."

He raised his head and gazed into her eyes. Even in the muted light of the nightclub she could see concern on his face. "But I'm not, Blair. Not in real life."

"I know you aren't." He looked so unhappy that

tenderness swept through Blair. Josh didn't seem to know how terrific he was. Almost instinctively, she placed her hand at the back of his neck, and drew his head down to hers. Without worrying about all the people watching them, she kissed him. She didn't care what everyone thought; in fact, she'd just as soon they knew. She was tired of pretending this man didn't mean something to her. He did—probably too much. But tonight, she didn't care if all of Raynes learned how she felt about Josh.

He was all wrong for her and common sense told her not to fall for him, but she couldn't help herself. She was falling in love with him, and she poured her love into her kiss. When Josh finally raised his head, they were both breathing hard.

"Wow," she murmured, leaning her head against his shoulder again. "I bet all of those cheerleaders you dated in high school taught you to kiss like that."

He'd been rubbing her back absently, but now his hand stilled. "I might have been the quarterback in high school, but I didn't date all the girls. I only had one girlfriend through all four years of high school, and I ended up proposing to her."

Blair tipped her head so she could see his face. He was serious. She could feel the tension in his body, the tightness in his muscles. With care, she kept her tone light. "You sure weren't like the quarterback in my high school. He chased all the pretty girls and caught most of them."

"You included?"

The slow song ended, and Blair reluctantly moved out of his arms. "No. I don't think I was pretty enough. He never even made a pass at me."

They had reached the table, but when she moved to sit, he stopped her. Smiling down at her, Josh said, "He was as much a fool as your ex-fiancé was."

Although Blair suspected he was only being polite, he still made her feel—terrific. Pretty and admired, something she hadn't felt in a long, long time. Until she'd met Josh, she hadn't realized how much her ego had been damaged when Marshall had left her. Josh made her feel like she was the only woman in the room. He might not love her, but she knew he cared about her. Plus, he'd always been truthful with her, a testimony to his character.

Glancing at her friends, she could tell from the expressions of the cast members they hadn't missed the kiss she'd shared with Josh on the dance floor. Blair sat next to Theresa, who looked like she was going to burst with excitement. When she met Blair's gaze, she winked, causing Blair to laugh.

Thankfully, before the inquisition could begin, Leigh returned to the table, her dance partner in tow.

"Everyone, this wonderful man is Mitch Houston. I believe I'm in love with him." She glanced at the older man, arching one well-shaped brow. "And whether he knows it or not, he's in love with me, too."

Mitch smiled at the group. "It's nice to meet all of you." He sat next to Leigh. One by one, the cast introduced themselves and their spouses. After Blair introduced herself, Mitch said to Josh, "You must be her husband."

Silence fell over the table, then Theresa laughed. "Guess you noticed the kiss these two shared on the dance floor. We've all been wondering about that." She looked at Blair. "Up until just a few minutes ago, we thought Blair and Josh were just friends. Guess we know now they're *really* good friends."

"Yep, that kiss sure looked friendly to me." Bob added a loud laugh to punctuate his words.

Blair felt warmth suffuse her cheeks. She shot a quick glance at Josh, who was watching her. No doubt he was waiting to see how she wanted to handle this situation. She wondered if he was thinking of the future, or what her life would be like after he left town. Would all of her friends feel sorry for her, especially since they knew her fiancé had left her in the past? It didn't really matter. If people decided to pity her, then so be it. Fear of the future wasn't a reason to miss out on spending this time with Josh.

"Josh is a tough man to resist," Blair finally said, picking up her now lukewarm soda and taking a sip.

"See, I knew he was the perfect Prince Charming."

Theresa glanced at her watch, then looked at her husband. "Speaking of Cinderella, I think it's about time we go home and spring the babysitter before she turns into a pumpkin."

Theresa's pronouncement made everyone at the table realize how late it was. The party broke up, and not a moment too soon for Blair. She wanted to get home so she could be alone with Josh. He'd taken his motorcycle, so he followed her home. As she drove, she glanced in the rearview mirror where she could see the headlight of the motorcycle.

There was so much she wanted to know about him, so many questions she'd like answered. Maybe tonight he'd tell her about himself. Hadn't he told her a little of his past on the dance floor? She'd been surprised he'd shared a small glimpse of his earlier life with her, and surprised by his confession: he'd proposed to his high school sweetheart. He didn't seem the type, but when it came right down to it, there was a lot she didn't know about Josh.

But she knew one thing—she cared deeply and that wasn't about to change.

Josh parked his motorcycle behind Blair's Mustang. As he removed his helmet, Blair came to stand next to the bike. Silently, they walked to the front door.

While she unlocked the door, she asked, "So you really dated the same girl throughout high school?"

He'd wondered if she was going to ask him about that. "Yes. Shelly and I were together for years."

Blair opened the door. "I think that's sweet—you knew from the beginning you were perfect for each other."

He could let her continue to think that. It would put an end to her questions. But the thought of deceiving Blair, even by omission, left a bitter taste in his mouth. He couldn't let her think he'd lived some sort of fairy tale.

"Shelly and I never really had a chance to decide if we were perfect together or not. Her parents and mine were close friends. We were put together from the time we could walk. I guess neither one of us ever questioned it, but we should have. We finally figured out later that we weren't in love."

He ran his hand through his hair, hating to crack open the past. Watching Blair closely, he reached around her and shut the door. "Have I totally killed the mood?"

"Oh, yeah, you know how we women hate it when a guy shares his feelings with us."

Josh chuckled. "Blair, I don't think—"

Suddenly, a child's scream sliced through the quiet of the night. Startled, Josh turned to unlock the front door. Yanking it open, he sprinted out into the yard. He glanced around, his heart slamming in his chest.

Then he saw a small figure perched on the top of Blair's roof and froze.

"Oh no. It's Melanie," Blair said by his side. She hollered up to the crying child. "Sweetie, don't move."

"I want to see the prince," the child said between tears. "My mom said the prince is staying here."

Prince? Josh's gut twisted. *The girl had crept out of her house and come over to see Prince Charming.* He had to do something quick. It was so dark, he could barely see the little girl.

"How did she get up there?" he muttered. Moving to the side of the house, he saw the answer to his question immediately. A metal extension ladder leaned against the house.

A wrenching sob tore from Blair. "The roofers left that ladder there last week. They promised me they'd come back and get it. I meant to move it. I just got busy and forgot."

Josh glanced at her and saw tears in her eyes. He patted her arm, but didn't want to talk about the ladder now. Instead, he needed Blair focused on the situation at hand. "Can you grab a flashlight?"

"Yes. And I'll bring the phone with me so we can call the police and her parents."

Without another word, Blair ran toward the front of the house. Josh looked up the length of the ladder, slightly illuminated by the full moon above them. He listened to the child crying, his heart breaking. *What had Blair said her name was—Melanie?*

"Melanie, sweetheart, are you holding on tightly?"

"My hands hurt . . ." She hiccupped a loud sob. "And I cut my knee. I think I'm going to fall."

Balling his hands into fists, he said, "It's going to be okay. Hold on."

Blair came running back, carrying a lantern and a flashlight. Without giving himself time to think, Josh said, "Hold the ladder and point the flashlight up there. I've got to get to the roof and make sure she's safe."

"Why don't I go up and get her?" Blair offered, heading toward the ladder.

He knew why she'd offered—because he disliked heights. But the thought of Blair climbing down that ladder with the little girl overcame any qualms he had.

"No. I'm going." He grabbed onto the ladder.

Blair didn't argue. She simply nodded. Before he could change his mind, Josh started climbing the ladder. Maybe it would have been wiser to wait for the police and fire department to arrive, but he couldn't risk it. Despite telling Melanie to stay still, he could hear her moving around. One wrong step and she'd fall.

So Josh kept climbing, pushing back the uneasiness he felt. It wasn't as difficult as he'd feared it might be. To comfort Melanie and take his own mind off his phobia, he asked the little girl, "What's your favorite toy?"

"Prince, is that you?" She let out a sob. "I'm scared."

"Don't worry. I'll be there in just a second, but I need you to stand still and don't move anymore." He heard her stop moving. Good—at least she wasn't heading toward the edge. "So you never told me, what's your favorite toy?"

"I have a lot of dolls, but Susie is my favorite. Are you the prince?" Her thin voice wavered with fear.

"I play Prince Charming, but I'm not really a prince. My name is Josh." He put one hand in front of the other, moving slowly forward. Fortunately, the ladder was steady against the side of the house. When he almost reached the top, he heard the wail of sirens in the distance. Blair must have called the police.

He climbed onto the roof, his heart in his throat. Melanie was only a few feet away. When she saw him, she stood up and started toward him on the slopping roof.

"No," Josh said. "Stand still. I'll come to you."

Melanie froze again. Slowly, carefully, Josh moved forward making certain he had a firm grip. Finally he was close enough to wrap his hand around Melanie's arm, bringing her over so he could secure her against him. He considered standing, but with Melanie, he had a better chance if he kept them low.

"Don't stand. You might fall." He forced a smile to cross his face. "Let's creep, okay?"

Melanie nodded. "Okay."

Below them, a couple of police cars and a fire truck arrived. They turned a bright floodlight on the ladder.

"Can you lead the child down?" a man hollered from below.

Could he lead her down? Josh looked at Melanie, who still had tears on her face. But beyond the tears, he could see the trust. She depended on him to get her out of this. No way would he let her down.

"Yeah. I can do it," Josh hollered back, smiling at Melanie. "Sweetie, we're going over to the ladder. Then we'll climb down slowly. Do you think you can do that?"

She bobbed her head, smiling back at him. "I'm a good climber."

"Yeah, I noticed." With care, he got them over to the edge of the roof and onto the ladder. He headed down the steps first, and then helped Melanie onto the ladder. But Josh didn't look down. He kept his focus firmly on Melanie.

"You won't let me fall, will you?" she asked.

His heart squeezed his chest. "I promise. I won't let you fall."

Slowly, step by step, they moved toward the ground. He was so focused on Melanie that he didn't really notice how far away from the ground they were.

From below, he heard a commotion when the child's parents arrived, but he didn't take his attention off Melanie. Finally, he stepped off the ladder and onto the ground.

With slightly shaky hands, he gathered the child close, hugging her. Pulling back to look at her face, he said, "Melanie, you must never do something like this again. You could have been hurt. Do you promise not to do it again?"

Melanie nodded solemnly. "I'm sorry."

Her parents gathered her up, crying and laughing and hugging her. Josh watched the scene, feeling the intense rush of relief. He wouldn't think about what could have happened if something had gone wrong. He couldn't stand the thought of that little girl getting hurt, in part because of him. She'd come looking for Prince Charming.

Blair ran over and wrapped her arms around his waist. "You were amazing," she said, hugging him tightly. His own arms seemed to wrap around her of their own volition. "I always knew you were a hero."

Josh didn't feel like a hero. He'd been scared the whole time, terrified Melanie would fall. "No, I'm not a hero. Trust me, I'm not."

Chapter Eight

Not a hero? How could he even think that? Blair sat on her front porch, watching the police complete their report with Josh. Even from this distance, she could hear the officers thanking him for rescuing Melanie. Everyone agreed he'd been terrific, except Josh.

It was crazy. And wrong. She knew he didn't like heights, yet he'd climbed that ladder without a second thought. Not once had he turned back. He did what needed to be done.

When it came right down to it, Prince Charming could learn a thing or two from Josh. Whether he thought so or not, he was a kind, thoughtful man, a man who had a strong heart and an even stronger code of ethics. Why else would he be playing the part of

Prince Charming in the first place? He'd done it for Eric, because they were friends, and Josh was loyal to his friends.

After a few more minutes, Josh shook the hands of the police officers and came over to where she sat.

"Hi there," she said, standing.

"Hi there, yourself."

Taking his hand, Blair headed toward the house, but Josh stopped her.

"Walk me to the garage," he said. "We've both had a long day, and I think it's best if we call it a night."

Blair figured he didn't want to talk right now, but she couldn't just let him go to the apartment without knowing how wonderful she thought he was. "You know, you really were amazing," she said as they walked. Before he could disagree, she continued, "You were. You went up the ladder and saved that child."

"Maybe, but I keep thinking that I was the reason she was on the roof in the first place."

"No, you weren't. As much as you'd like to blame this on yourself, the only one who put Melanie on the roof was Melanie. She climbed up all by herself. All you did was save her."

They had reached the outside stairs leading to the garage apartment, and Josh sat. "I just wish I'd done things differently."

Blair sat on the narrow step next to him. Two porch lights from the back of her house gave them a little light, but she couldn't quite see his face clearly. She wished she could, because she wanted to know what was going on in his mind.

"What could you have done differently? You didn't put a sign outside advertising free pictures with Prince Charming if they climbed up on the roof."

"Yeah, you're right, but what if she'd fallen?"

Blair leaned toward him, bumping their shoulders. "Melanie didn't fall because you saved her. Plain and simple. You saved that child."

"I guess I know that in my head, but it's difficult not to feel responsible."

Hoping to cheer him up, she said, "There's a rumor going around that not everything that happens is your fault. You can't control the world."

He smiled but remained silent for a long time. Finally, Blair asked the question preying on her mind. "What happened with Shelly?"

"I'm not sure—"

"You don't have to tell me. I realize it's private."

Josh smiled ruefully, then said, "I proposed to Shelly when I got out of the Army, I think because everyone expected us to get married. To tell you the truth, I'd come home to figure out what I wanted to do with my life. Shelly was still single, and everyone in town expected us to pick up where we'd left off: the high school football star and the cheerleader. So we sort of fell into an engagement. We were young."

"What happened?" Blair asked softly.

"After I proposed, our families were thrilled. The whole town seemed to get caught up in the wedding plans. Everyone was happy."

Her heart felt for the young man he'd been. "But you weren't happy."

"Don't get me wrong, in a way I was excited. Sure, I had some doubts, but Shelly and I had been together most of our lives. I figured it would work out."

"But it didn't."

He sighed. "As the wedding grew closer, we started to fight a lot. Shelly wanted me to work at her father's construction company, and I wanted to go to college. I'd always been fascinated by computers. After a while, I started taking night classes at the local college. Shelly was really upset, but I felt I could provide us with a better future if I went to college."

Blair's heart went out to him. She knew how hard it was to do what you felt you had to in life when the people around you didn't support your dreams. "What ended up happening?"

He ran one hand across his face. "We both finally sat down, and agreed to call it off. Last I heard, Shelly married a man who worked at her father's company and they have two children. So as you can see, I'm hardly Prince Charming."

"Josh, it wasn't your fault. Sometimes relationships don't work out. Mine didn't either. Even if you hadn't gone to college, you and Shelly probably wouldn't have lasted."

"That's just it. I'm sure it wouldn't have lasted. No one in my family is successful in marriage. We aren't the happily-ever-after kind."

Blair studied him for a moment, uncertain what to say. Finally she asked, "How did your family react to your broken engagement?"

"My father didn't say a word. My mother laughed and said she wasn't surprised. And that was the end of that."

He stood, then faced her. "I guess forever isn't in my DNA." Leaning down, he lightly brushed a kiss across her temple. When he moved back, Blair met his gaze. "Have a nice night, Blair. I'll see you tomorrow."

"Yeah. Tomorrow." She stood so Josh could climb the stairs. After a second, she headed back inside her house, thinking about what he'd told her. He had a broken engagement in his past, too. And all of the marriages in his family had failed. *Forever wasn't in his DNA,* he'd said.

Which meant Josh really was all wrong for her, since forever was exactly what she wanted in her life. She wanted a marriage that would truly last for all eternity.

But if Josh was so very wrong for her, then why did this thing between them feel so very right?

* * *

"Well, if it isn't our resident hero." Bob Julian moved into the dressing room, grinning. He slapped Josh hard on the back. "I'm proud of you. You did a good job saving that little girl."

Slightly embarrassed, Josh glanced in the mirror, checking his costume. Idly, he straightened a couple of the medals. He should be used to the fussing by now. His whole day had been like this, people coming to the house to thank him for saving Melanie. They'd all been sincere in their thanks, making it clear they really did appreciate what he'd done. The attention was flattering, but also made him uncomfortable. He'd done what anyone would do. That hardly made him a hero.

Not that he'd had any luck convincing the people from town. Throughout the day, neighbors and friends had dropped off an assortment of baked goods. By the time he and Blair had left for the auditorium, Josh had enough pastries to hold his own bake sale.

"I didn't do anything special," Josh said for the twentieth time today. "You would have done the same thing."

Bob's loud laugh filled the small room. "No way. Look at me, son. I'm way too big to shimmy up a ladder. I'd have had to send the missus up there. She weighs about half of what I do." He patted his rotund stomach as if to emphasize his point.

Josh chuckled and went to move around the older man. "You would have figured out a way to help Melanie."

Although the play wasn't due to start for a few more minutes, Josh wanted a chance to wish Blair good luck. He hadn't had much time alone with her today. As much as he hated to admit it, he would have loved to spend the day alone with her. But the well-wishers prevented that.

Before Josh could open the door, Bob stopped him again. "Mind if we talk for a moment?"

Something in the other man's voice made Josh tense. "I guess not."

Bob said, "I won't dance around. You're a smart man, Josh, so I guess you've figured out by now that folks in Raynes think the world of Blair. She's a really sweet lady." He ran one finger around his collar. "The thing is, she's got a heart as big as the Grand Canyon. That fiancé already did a real number on her. All of us sure would hate to see her hurt again."

Josh was beyond tense by now. Truthfully, he was worried about the same thing. But the words sounded different coming from Bob's mouth. More real. More true. He knew Blair had feelings for him, and he couldn't help wondering how she was going to feel after he left town.

"I'm not going to hurt her," Josh said, wishing he could be as certain as he sounded.

Bob scratched his chin. "That's the thing. You probably don't mean to hurt her, but come on, this is Blair. You really think you're not going to break her heart when you hop on your motorcycle and breeze out of town? I saw the way she kissed you last night. Blair's stuck on you."

Josh leveled his gaze on the other man. In the space of a few seconds, Bob had reminded him of the flipside of all the concern you got in a small town: people didn't hesitate to comment on your behavior. "Don't you think this is something Blair and I should talk about?"

Bob wasn't the least offended. He shrugged and opened the door. "Maybe. But people here in Raynes look out for each other. And as her friend, I thought I should say something."

The older man headed across the stage, leaving Josh to trail after him. A few of the actors came over to praise him for saving Melanie. But while they talked, Josh's mind was on his conversation with Bob. He made it obvious that Blair's friends were worried he was going to hurt her.

Unfortunately, he didn't know how not to hurt her. He'd told her time and again what sort of man he really was. Yet he could feel that she cared for him in her sweet kisses and her gentle touch.

So what was he supposed to do now? His gut told him to leave tonight, to head out to L.A. before he made things worse. But he couldn't do that. Blair was depending on him to finish the play, and he cared about her too much to leave her in the lurch.

But there was more to his feelings than just concern. These days, he spent most of his time thinking about her, wanting to be with her. But he wouldn't let his feelings deepen beyond caring, and Blair understood that. He'd been honest with her from the beginning. She knew he wasn't the forever type.

After he left, Blair would be better off. She'd be able to find the right man, a man who could offer her everything she wanted in life.

So if he was doing the right thing, then why did he feel like he was taking advantage of the best woman he'd ever known?

By the time they got home from the performance, Blair figured it wasn't humanly possibly to be happier than she was. She and Josh had stopped at the grocery store, and now they carried the bags inside the house, laughing as they went. Every time she looked at Josh, her feelings for him grew. He was downright perfect.

Too bad it would all end in a few days.

Pushing that thought away, she set her bag on the kitchen counter and grabbed the ringing phone. Blair smiled as she watched Josh head back out to her car. She could get used to this, but she wouldn't. If she wasn't careful, this domestic moment might lull her into thinking she could change his mind, but she knew better. He would be leaving soon and that was that.

"Blair, it's Dad."

Blair's heart slammed in her chest. Her father rarely called. Something had to be wrong. "What's up?"

Her father laughed. "Don't sound so worried. I'm fine."

"I wasn't worried." It was truly amazing—no matter how old Blair got, she still felt like she was five years old when she spoke to her father. Especially these days. Ever since Marshall had jilted her, her father treated her like she was a china doll, capable of shattering at any moment. Nothing Blair said ever seemed to win back his confidence in her.

"I wanted to let you know I've decided to come for a visit next Saturday. I'd like to see Eric. Plus I can see the play you're directing."

"Really?"

"Of course."

Talk about amazing. Ever since her father had retired from the service, he'd become a golf fanatic and hated to be away from his hobby for too long. If Raynes had a golf course, Blair knew he would stop by to check it out. But there was no golf course, which meant he really *was* coming to see his children.

"That's great." Just then Josh came in, carrying the remaining grocery bags. He smiled at her, and began putting the food away. Josh. He would still be here when her dad arrived. In fact, next Saturday would be his last day in town. Blair had always assumed they'd go out with the cast after the final performance to celebrate the play. Then she hoped the two of them could have a private celebration, maybe go dancing or something. She knew Josh intended to leave for California early Sunday morning.

But now the private celebration wouldn't happen. Still, she loved her father and she was looking forward to seeing him.

As she listened to her dad, Blair watched Josh moving around her kitchen, glancing at her from time to time. Her father was talking about the trip, but Blair's mind wasn't on the conversation. Instead, it was firmly focused on how much she would miss Josh after he left. She didn't want to love Josh, but looking at him now and thinking of life without him made her realize how deep her love for him really was.

A new—and terrible—thought occurred to her: her father was going to be around immediately after Josh left. He'd be here during those first tough days when her heart would feel like it was breaking.

No way could she let her father see her hurt again by another man leaving. She'd have to pretend her heart wasn't breaking, which would be the performance of her life.

Because there was no way around it—when Josh left town, he would take her heart with him.

* * *

Josh finished unpacking the groceries while Blair wrapped up her phone conversation. Once done, he started to leave the kitchen so she could have privacy, but she shook her head, making it clear she didn't mind if he stayed.

So he started dinner, trying not to listen in on her call. But he was six feet from her; how could he not hear what she said?

Her father was coming to visit, that much was obvious. And although Blair was saying how excited she was by the visit, Josh could tell from her tense stance that something was bothering her. He waited until Blair hung up the phone, then leaned against the counter and studied her.

"My dad is coming," she said after a few moments.

He nodded, still watching Blair closely. No doubt about it, she felt unsettled. She paced the kitchen, idly straightening things that were already tidy.

"Will you be happy to see him?" he asked.

Blair stopped, turning to face him. "Sure. My father and I get along fairly well these days."

"So what's the problem?"

At first he thought Blair might ignore his question, but after releasing a heartfelt sigh, she said, "He's arriving on Saturday to see Eric and to catch the last performance of the play." She shot a quick look at him, then glanced away. "I was hoping we might go out to dinner or something that last evening."

Suddenly, it all made sense—she wanted to be alone with him his last night in town.

"That's no problem. What do you say I take you to dinner a couple of times before then?" He came to stand next to Blair, dropping his arm around her shoulders. *Josh, the woman was tense.* "Does that work?"

"You wouldn't mind?"

He smiled. "Um, no. I *don't* mind taking a pretty woman to dinner." He rubbed one shoulder and added, "Can I do anything to help you get ready for his visit?"

"No. There's nothing you can do."

Josh wrapped his arms loosely around her waist, tugging her a little closer. "Tell me what's bothering you."

She sighed deeply. "It's all ending so soon, and it's been so wonderful."

He knew she wasn't talking about the play. She was talking about their time together. She was right—their time together had been wonderful. Unlike anything he'd ever experienced.

He turned to her and studied her upturned face, losing himself for a moment in her deep gaze. Without fanfare, he suddenly knew he loved her. Loved her deeply and completely. Expectantly, he waited for panic to settle over him, but instead he felt only emptiness at the thought of never seeing Blair again.

The words felt like a knife to his soul: *why did things have to be like this? Why couldn't they be different?* He considered the idea again. *Why couldn't they be different?*

Maybe they could keep seeing each other even after he left for L.A. He could talk to his new boss, Ed Pattinola, about traveling back to Raynes every three to four weeks for a visit. Lots of contractors took one long weekend off a month. He knew maintaining a long-distance romance would be difficult, but wasn't Blair worth it?

"I didn't mean to upset you," Blair said.

"I'm not upset." Looking at her with love in his heart, he couldn't help thinking a better man would walk away from her now. A better man wouldn't expect her to put aside her dreams of a home and family to spend time with him.

"I'm selfish," he admitted, mostly directing the words to himself. "I like being with you."

He really was selfish. He knew Blair loved him, he could see it in her eyes, feel it in her touch. If he asked, she'd probably say yes, she'd make do with seeing him only occasionally.

But was it fair to ask her?

He was still wrestling with the problem when Blair said, "Being with you makes me happy, too."

Indecision flooded Josh. *Was it fair to ask her to see him only once a month?* Could they really continue things long-distance after he left? Before Saturday, he'd have to decide whether he should ask her.

But he wouldn't decide right now. Instead, he suggested, "I have an idea. Why don't we make tonight memorable? I'll take you out to dinner at the fanciest restaurant in Raynes."

"Mr. Anderson, are you trying to lead me astray?" Blair asked with a smile.

Josh chuckled. "Sweetheart, you have no idea."

"So, you think you'll survive after he leaves?" Theresa asked, dropping into the chair next to Blair's. They had about twenty minutes before tonight's performance would begin. The rest of the cast was busy dressing, but Theresa was ready.

Despite the casual tone of her question, Theresa's expression was sympathetic. With a groan, Blair realized it had started already—people in town felt sorry for her, and Josh hadn't even left yet. It was only Friday. Josh wouldn't leave until after the performance tomorrow; they still had a few more hours together.

"I'm fine, Theresa, and I'm going to continue to be fine," Blair said, knowing in a way it was true. Josh's leaving would hurt, there was no doubt about that. But over the last few days she'd decided that the joy she'd experienced with Josh was worth the sadness she'd feel after he left. In a way, it was like buying the car. In the past, she'd always followed the safe road. But look where that had landed her with Marshall—she'd still ended up with heartache. This time, she followed her heart, but at least she knew the rules going in. Sure, she'd be sad after Josh left, but she would survive.

"You're such a liar," Theresa said. "And a bad liar at that. You're in love with him, and you're going to be miserable when he leaves."

There was no sense pretending, so Blair admitted, "Yes, I am in love with him, but I've known all along he was leaving."

"Oh, honey, when it became obvious you two were falling for each other, I'd hoped maybe Josh had changed his mind about leaving."

The sadness on Theresa's face tugged at Blair's heart. Refusing to be a baby, she forced herself to remain in control. "No, nothing's changed. After the performance tomorrow, Josh will be gone."

Theresa sighed. "Have you at least talked to him about your feelings? You've told him you love him, right? You've asked him to change his mind?" She leaned forward in her chair. "You're at least going to try to stop him from leaving, right?"

"Of course not." Blair glanced around the stage. The activity level was increasing. She needed to make final preparations for the play to start.

"You, my girl, are a wimp," Theresa announced. "A dyed in the wool, full-fledged, card-carrying wimp."

She raised one arched brow. "And I mean that in the kindest way possible."

Indignant, Blair looked at her friend. "I am not a wimp. I'm a realist. I know Josh doesn't want to live in a town like Raynes, and to tell you the truth, I don't want to waste my time with a man who doesn't share my dreams. Okay, I love him. And sure, I'm going to miss him when he goes. But I'll survive."

And she would. Life didn't make any promises, and the memories of her time with Josh would be with her forever. Someday in the future, she was certain she'd find a man who wanted a settled life. When she did, she'd appreciate him all the more. She'd understand that finding the right partner was something truly magical to be cherished.

"I'm not a wimp," Blair maintained again. "But I won't make Josh unhappy by asking him to stay. I love him enough not to kill his dreams."

"Ha! He should be so lucky as to have a great woman like you in his life. You shouldn't give up."

Slowly, Blair shook her head. Theresa just wouldn't understand. The job in L.A. meant a lot to Josh's career plans. He had a golden opportunity there, one he couldn't lose. Blair wanted him to have his dream, she wanted him to be happy.

Wasn't that what love was about?

Turning to face Theresa, Blair said, "I'm not giving

up. For all I know, Josh doesn't love me in return. I know when to let go."

Theresa stood and looked at Blair. "Seems to me you could use a few lessons in hanging on."

Josh looked at himself in the dressing room mirror, then quickly turned away. He still hadn't asked Blair about having a long-distance relationship, and time was running out.

The bottom line was, he wasn't sure it was fair to her. Turning it over in his mind some more, Josh wandered out onto the stage. He could see Blair across the way, talking to Theresa. After a moment, she looked his way and smiled. As always, her smile cut straight to his heart, but these days there was more than a hint of sadness in her smile. He knew she dreaded tomorrow. He dreaded it, too. He hated seeing her upset, especially since he knew he was the cause of her sadness.

Blair was still smiling at him. Josh smiled back. Tonight, when they got back to her house, he'd mention the possibility of seeing each other occasionally. He had to see if Blair felt the same way he did—that seeing each other once in a while was better than not seeing each other at all.

A long-distance relationship might not be the perfect solution, but it was the only one he could come up with.

*   *   *

"Talk about a nightmare," Theresa muttered as she came to stand next to Blair halfway through the performance. "I can't think of anything that hasn't gone wrong tonight."

Blair nodded slowly. Theresa was right. Everything that could go wrong, had gone wrong. So far, three major props couldn't be found and both Leigh and Bob kept flubbing their lines. Blair didn't know whether she wanted to scream, cry, or laugh.

Deep down, though, she knew the problems with the play weren't the only things bothering her. Her talk with Theresa had left her jumpy. It had driven home the fact that Josh was leaving tomorrow, and she hadn't even told him that she loved him.

"Do you think the audience has noticed the problems?" Theresa asked.

Blair pulled her attention away from the stage for a moment and looked at her friend. "The only way we'll be okay is if everyone spontaneously falls asleep."

Theresa chuckled. "Oh, good. Then we still have a chance."

Despite all the trouble, Blair smiled. "Yeah. Maybe."

Glancing back at the stage, she groaned when Leigh forgot yet another line. This time Josh helped cover the awkward silence. As always, when he was around Blair couldn't stop herself from watching him. He was so tall and handsome any woman would find him attractive. But Blair loved him for more than his good looks. She loved the way he cared, the way he made everyone around him feel good about themselves.

Whether Josh liked to admit it or not, he truly was a hero. He'd proven it to her over and over again. Even tonight, he was coming to Leigh's rescue, and when one of the doors on the set started to fall off, he'd simply walked over and removed it like the faulty scenery was part of the play.

The man was . . . Blair sighed. *He was perfect.*

The last few days had been difficult. They'd worked furiously to get her house ready for her dad's visit. Now, thanks to Josh, Blair's new house looked phenomenal. Not at all like the ramshackle fixer-upper she'd bought a few short weeks ago.

All she wanted now was to be alone with him. To listen to his outrageous tales of his childhood and to hear him laugh. But that wasn't going to happen if tonight's performance didn't end. When Leigh forgot her lines yet again, Theresa sighed.

"Looks like Leigh's falling for that new boyfriend of hers," Theresa said.

"Why do you say that?"

Theresa grinned. "Being in love has a way of making even the most sane person flustered and forgetful—just like you."

"I'm not forgetful," Blair said, watching the stage closely. Bob tripped over a prop.

"Too bad. Being forgetful could come in handy for you over the next couple of months." She patted Blair's arm. "I'll come over tomorrow after the performance and hold your hand. I know you're going to be sad."

Blair wanted to argue with her friend, but she knew it was hopeless. She would be sad. "I'll be okay. My dad is arriving in the morning."

"Wow. One look at you, and he'll know you're in love with Josh. Do you think he'll give you a hard time about it?"

If it was that obvious, her dad would certainly realize she was in love with Josh. And if it was obvious, did Josh know she loved him? Possibly. Okay, probably. He was a smart man. No doubt he'd known for a long time.

Glancing out at the stage, she watched Josh dance with Leigh. It didn't matter if he knew she loved him. In some ways, she wanted him to know. Not so it would hurt him, but because she hoped someday he'd come to realize how terrific she thought he was.

Blair's vision blurred, and she was surprised to realize she was on the verge of tears. With effort, she blinked them away. She wouldn't cry. Not tonight, their last night together. Tonight, she would savor every second she had with Josh.

Tomorrow would be soon enough for her heart to break.

Chapter Nine

"You know, I think this place looks pretty spectacular," Blair said, wandering out onto the back porch. They'd had dinner as soon as they arrived home from the play. Afterward, she volunteered to do the dishes since he cooked. Deciding to finish a few things on the back porch, he came outside. Since it was too late to hammer, he settled on painting the only section of railing he'd replaced so far.

Blair came to stand next to him, a smile on her face. "Although it's sweet of you to work on my house, it isn't necessary."

"I don't mind helping."

"Still, it seems wrong for you to work on the house

150

considering you already cooked dinner on your last night in town."

Josh turned to look at her. She looked so pretty and sweet under the overhead light. Whether it was the right thing to do or not, he wanted to keep her in his life.

"I've been meaning to talk to you about something," he said before he could change his mind.

"What?"

There was a breathless hitch in her voice, almost as if she realized what he intended on asking her. "I know I'm all set to leave tomorrow, but maybe we could still see each other occasionally. You know, date."

Confusion crossed her face. "I don't understand how—you'll be in Los Angeles."

"I thought I might come visit now and again."

Blair had reached the far side of the porch. Now she turned and looked at him, a frown wrinkling her forehead. "Visit?"

Josh replaced the lid on the can of paint and then faced Blair. "Yeah. I might be able to convince my manager to let me have a couple of days off once a month."

His words seemed to hang in the air. He could tell he'd surprised her. A lump of doubt settled beneath his breastbone while he waited for her reaction.

Finally, Blair moved forward a couple steps. "And you'd come here."

Josh studied her closely, unable to tell what she was thinking. "Yeah. I could fly back to visit."

"Visit?"

He smiled. "Honey, either I've stunned you or you've forgotten how to talk."

Blair didn't return his smile. She just stood there, staring at him. He knew she was debating his offer. He also knew the arrangement wasn't what she wanted . . . not really.

When she blinked and looked away from him, he half-suspected there were tears in her eyes. "I don't know what to say," she said softly.

"Why don't you think about it? We don't have to decide right now." His voice sounded rougher than he intended, but he couldn't help being disappointed. He wanted to her say yes.

"Why do you want to keep seeing me?" Blair asked softly as she leaned her weight against one of the older sections of the railing. Before Josh could warn her the wood there was rotten, the railing broke. With a yelp, she tumbled off the porch, crashing onto the hard ground.

Josh felt his heart slam in his chest with worry.

"Blair, are you okay?" He jumped to the ground. As much as he wanted to gather her into his arms, he didn't want to move her until he knew the extent of her injury. A quick inspection showed she had a nasty cut on her forehead. Before he could stop her, Blair sat up, blood leaving a thin trail down the side of her face. Slowly, she stood. Josh helped her steady herself.

"Well, that was coordinated." She dabbed at her forehead with her fingers.

"Let's go inside so I can see how bad this cut is." With one hand around her waist and the other holding her elbow, Josh helped her up the porch stairs and into the kitchen. He felt like his gut was tied in a square knot. He loved this woman—seeing her hurt like this tore him to pieces.

Gently, he sat her in a kitchen chair, then cleaned the wound. Even with his limited first-aid training, he could tell she needed stitches. After finding some clean gauze pads, he created a makeshift bandage, wishing all the while that he'd moved faster and caught her before she fell.

"Keep that on the cut." Instinctively he made a move for his keys, then realized Blair wasn't in any shape to ride on a motorcycle. "Where are your keys?"

"Why?" She kept the pad pressed firmly against her forehead, yet blood still trickled down the side of her face.

At the sight of her blood, Josh said, "I need to drive you to the hospital."

Blair looked for a moment like she might argue, but

apparently thought better of it. "Okay. I guess I could use a couple of stitches."

Josh nodded and helped her stand. Slowly, they headed toward the car. After he helped Blair settle into the passenger's seat, he climbed in the driver's side. As he headed toward the hospital, he glanced at her. The flow of blood had slowed to a trickle.

"It looks better now," he said, trying to reassure her.

Blair gave him a weak smile. "Thank goodness you were here tonight to help me."

Josh froze. Yeah—he'd been here tonight. But he wouldn't be around the next time Blair needed him.

Once they got to the emergency room the wait seemed forever. The small hospital was overflowing with patients, so after a quick check by a nurse who determined she wasn't bleeding too badly, Blair settled down next to Josh.

Josh started to pace. Fortunately, before he could wear a rut into the floor, a nurse led Blair to an examination room. Josh came with her, which was just as well—Blair was a bit of a coward when it came to hospitals.

A tall gray-haired woman entered the room, a smile on her face. "Hi, Blair. You trying to out-do Eric?"

Blair returned the woman's smile. "Hi, Renee. I don't think my injuries come anywhere near his." She glanced at Josh. "Josh, this is Dr. Renee Culvert. I'm her accountant. Renee, this is Josh Anderson."

Renee leaned over and studied Blair's cut. "Are you the guy playing Prince Charming in Blair's play?" she asked while she worked on Blair's wound.

"Yes," Josh said.

Blair bit back a smile. Josh hovered directly over Renee's shoulder, closely watching her every move.

"Does it look bad?" he asked the doctor.

Renee shook her head. "Not really, although Blair, you're probably going to have a little scar here when it's all done."

Blair tensed as the older woman began working on her forehead. Although Renee was gentle, Blair couldn't seem to relax. Josh must have noticed her tension because he came up on the side of the table and patted her hand until Renee shooed him away. His gesture touched her more than she could say.

"I thought only the actors playing Prince Charming got hurt—first Eric, then Kyle. Blair, you'd think as the director you would've been safe. What happened?" Renee asked.

Blair, briefly explained how she'd fallen through the railing on the back porch.

"So Prince Charming came to the rescue again. Good thing Josh is staying at Eric's place so he could drive you here," Renee said.

"How did you know?" Josh asked.

Renee chuckled. "This is a small town. *Everyone* knows everything." She gave Blair a pointed look. "Everyone seems to find it very interesting, too. Especially since you're a handy guy to have around in case of emergency."

An awkward silence fell on the room. Blair would have given anything to know what Josh was thinking.

"Truthfully, I'm probably about as handy as an ant at a picnic—more an annoyance than a help," he said.

Although Renee laughed at his comment, something in Josh's voice struck Blair as odd. Surely he couldn't believe that he wasn't a help to her. She wanted to look at him, but she couldn't move. *Did Josh think he could have somehow prevented the accident?* Or worse, did he think that after tomorrow, he wouldn't be around the next time she needed him?

Well, he wouldn't be, even if she agreed to his idea of a long-distance relationship. *What had he said? That he could come to Raynes once a month for a visit. They could date.* But could she make do with that, with only seeing him occasionally?

Truthfully, she wasn't certain. All she knew was she wanted to get out of this hospital quickly. She didn't want to spend the last few hours she might have with Josh in the emergency room.

Renee leaned back, surveying Blair's forehead. "There you go. Four brand-new stitches to show the neighbors. Everyone is going to want to see the wound when they hear how Josh was around to rescue yet another damsel-in-distress."

Closing her eyes, Blair bit back a groan. Renee didn't mean any harm, but her words probably only made Josh feel worse. Anxious to leave, Blair asked, "Am I set to go?"

Renee quickly gave her a list of instructions on caring for the wound and told her when to return to have the stitches removed. Then the doctor turned and shook Josh's hand.

"It's been a pleasure meeting you," Renee told him. "Looks like Blair picked the right man to play Prince Charming."

With a quick smile at Blair, the doctor left the room. Blair looked at Josh, but could tell nothing from his expression.

"Let's get out of here," she said, moving to climb off the examination table. Josh came over and helped her down. For just a second, she felt a tiny bit wobbly, but the sensation quickly passed. She thought about going upstairs to check on Eric, but since it was well after visiting hours, she'd wait until tomorrow.

On the way to her car, she smiled at Josh, her heart in her throat. "Well, this has been an interesting evening. Between the problems during the performance and spending the rest of the night in the emergency room, we didn't have much of a chance to enjoy our last night together."

Josh opened the passenger's door and helped her into the car, then climbed into the driver's seat.

She could tell in the faint light from the dash how upset he was. She felt her love for him tug at her heart. As far as she could tell, the best way to deal with this problem was head-on.

Turning slightly in her seat, she studied him. "My fall is not your fault, so stop blaming yourself."

"What makes you think I'm blaming myself?"

"You're not?"

He kept his attention fixed on the road. "I guess not, but I think I could have done things differently."

"Like what? I saw you working on the railing, but I leaned against it anyway. I fell. It was *my* fault. End of subject. But you can do something differently now—you can decide not to ruin the remaining hours we have left by punishing yourself."

He didn't respond to her words. Instead, he asked, "How are you feeling?"

"I'm fine," she assured him. "I feel like the klutz of the century, but other than that, I'm fine." She reached over and laid her hand on his arm. "I really am fine, Josh, so you can stop frowning. I hate to tell you this, but that wasn't the first time I've fallen, and it won't be the last. A few measly stitches are no big deal."

"But what if I hadn't been there to help you?" he asked as he pulled into the driveway, turning off the car.

"Then I would have found a different way to the hospital." With a smile she added, "But just for the record, you *were* more help than an ant at a picnic."

Josh leaned back in his seat and studied Blair. She was smiling at him, trying to convince him she was okay. Intellectually, he knew she was fine, but in his gut, he felt like walls were closing in on him. He'd lived this scene before when he let Shelley down. He didn't want to do the same thing to Blair.

"I've thought it over, and I don't think we should keep seeing each other after I leave for L.A.," he said, feeling pain as he spoke those words but knowing that he was doing the right thing.

Blair's smile faded and she sighed. "Can we talk about this tomorrow? I'm not really up to it right now."

Since he loved Blair, Josh wasn't about to let her settle for less than her dream of a family and a life in Raynes. But she was tired, and she was right—they could talk this over in the morning.

"Sure." But he knew he wasn't going to change his mind. He loved Blair too much to let her settle for less. And unfortunately, that was all he had to offer.

Blair woke with a start, her heart pounding with fear. For a second, she was consumed by a wave of panic. Then slowly, the reality of her room seeped through and she started to calm down. She couldn't remember what she'd been dreaming, but based on how frightened she'd been, she could guess.

Josh. In a few hours he would be gone from her life. Blair sighed and sat up, drawing her knees under her. When they got home from the hospital, he said he didn't think they should see each other after he left for L.A. She could probably change his mind, but how could she see Josh only once a month . . . or even less? Sure, she could do it for a while. But what about a year from now? Or two? Josh had made it clear he didn't intend to settle down. That meant having a long-distance relationship with him would only be postponing the inevitable. Sooner of later, she'd have to let him go.

Maybe he was right. Maybe they should just forget the whole idea and end things now. Love for him filled her, but was love enough? It didn't give her the right to ask him to change his mind. And to be honest, she didn't want to settle for less than a man who wanted the same things she did.

For too many years, she'd dreamt of belonging somewhere, surrounding by people who cared about her. Her aunt hadn't cared. She'd made it clear she viewed Blair as a burden. Blair knew her father cared about her in his own way, but their relationship wasn't a close one. She wasn't part of his life any more than he was part of hers.

She still clearly remembered the day her father had told her he was sending her to stay with her aunt. A teenaged girl needed a female in her life, he'd said. Eric, naturally, would stay with him. They'd visit her often, so there was no reason for her to be upset. Even though they wouldn't see each other a lot, Blair would know her father and brother loved her.

At first, Blair had looked forward to their visits. But after a while, she couldn't help wishing they wouldn't come anymore. The visits upset her. They reminded her of the normal life she'd lost when her mother died.

A long-distance relationship with Josh would be the same way. At first, she'd look forward to his visits. But eventually, seeing the man she loved only a few days out of each year would only remind her of what she was missing. He was right—she couldn't live like that. Tomorrow, she would have to tell him goodbye.

The next morning, Blair walked down the stairs slowly, refusing to give into threatening tears. She would not cry today. Tears might make Josh feel guilty, which was the last thing she wanted to do. No, she had to be an adult about this. Sometimes certain people just weren't meant to be together. As painful as it was, she knew she wasn't meant to be with Josh.

She had to accept that fact. Wishing life could be different didn't make it so. And love didn't give you the right to destroy the dreams and plans of the other

person. The kind of love Blair believed in was sup-
portive, nurturing. Not destructive.

Someday, she'd find the right man and they'd build
a life together. But that day wouldn't be today. And
that man wouldn't be Josh. Sure, she knew he cared
about her. He might even love her. But he wasn't right
for her.

Blair tacked a smile firmly on her face and headed
across the backyard to Eric's apartment. Josh unlocked
the door following her knock. He was talking on the
phone. He smiled at her as she entered the apartment.
His smile had a sadness to it that was no doubt re-
flected in her own. He waved her over to his side, and
inspected the bandage on her forehead while he listened to the person on the other end of the phone.

"I figure I should be there Wednesday," he said into
the receiver. "Yeah. I'm looking forward to it, too. I
appreciate this opportunity."

Listening to his words, Blair refused to be de-
pressed. She should be happy for Josh. This programming contract was a real coup for him. Still, it was an
effort to stand there, listening to him tell the person
on the other end how anxious he was to get to Los
Angeles. Oh, she knew he didn't mean the words personally. He wasn't running away from her, not the
way Marshall had. He was going toward his future.

So she forced herself to tuck the hurt into a little

corner of her heart, somewhere far away where it wouldn't spoil her last day with this man.

After Josh finished his conversation and hung up the phone, he studied her, his expression serious. "I think we need to talk about us."

Knowing he was right, Blair went over to the kitchen table and sat, steeling herself. "Sure. Let's talk."

Josh grabbed his coffee cup off the counter. Nodding toward the pot, he asked, "Want some? I can't believe you can have a decent conversation in the morning without caffeine."

She was already way too jittery, so she shook her head. "I'm fine."

Josh settled in the chair across from her, his gaze fixed for several long moments on his coffee mug. When he finally looked up at her, he wore the same sad expression he'd had when she first entered the kitchen.

Leaning toward her, he said, "Did I ever tell you my father was the mayor of Massey Falls, the town where I grew up?"

Blair shook her head. "No."

"Well, he was. Every time an election rolled around, Dad would be elected again. Once or twice, someone ran against him, but most of the time, no one even tried. My father was incredibly popular with the people in town. He'd been the quarterback in high school, married the prom queen, opened a local business and helped pump money into the community."

"A hometown hero?"

"Oh, yeah, for a while. Until his first couple of marriages fell apart. Then the folks in town weren't too crazy about him. The same thing happened with my mom. Her friends sort of drifted away. But no matter what my mom and dad did, all of their relationships seemed doomed. But that didn't stop either of them from pushing Shelly at me."

A clearer picture of his childhood formed in Blair's mind. "Why?"

His laughter was hollow. "I'm not really sure. But they thought it would be a great idea if we got married. I guess like the rest of the town, they expected us to fall in love. Maybe in their own way they thought the town would accept them again if I married Shelly. I felt kind of guilty when things didn't work out."

"I think most children feel they need to live up to the expectations of their parents," Blair said softly.

"I know. They do. And so did I, for a while. But after we called off the engagement, I learned how quickly people can turn against you when you don't live up to those expectations."

"The people in town?"

"Yeah. But what really bothered me was despite the fact that my parents had wanted me to marry Shelly, they didn't seem at all surprised when our engagement ended. I think they knew all along I had the same rotten luck the two of them had when it came to love."

A bad feeling settled over Blair. "You don't really believe that, do you? Their broken marriages aren't about luck."

Josh blew out a breath. "I'm not so sure, Blair. I really believe some people just don't have what it takes to make love last."

Blair felt tears gather in her eyes. "Oh, Josh. Don't you think you can *work* at love to make it last?"

"I've never seen much evidence of that."

Blair sighed. "You can't go through life thinking you're incapable of making a relationship work. If you do, you'll always be alone."

Uncertainty showed clearly in Josh's eyes. "Blair, the reason I told you this was so you would understand why I can't stay in Raynes with you. This small-town lifestyle isn't for me." His smiled wanly. "Not that you've asked me to stay."

His quiet voice pierced straight to her heart. "I'd ask you if I thought you could," she said softly.

"And I'd ask you to come with me if I thought you could." His smile was sad. "But you couldn't, could you, Blair? You couldn't spend your life moving from town to town."

He was right. That sort of life would eat at her very soul. She couldn't go through that again. Not even for Josh.

Liz Thompson

"I couldn't do it," she admitted to him. "I hated my life growing up, and now that I've finally found a place where I belong, I can't simply walk away. I wish I could. You have no idea how I wish I could. But I know I can't. I'm sorry."

"I know, honey. I understand, and I'd never want to make you unhappy. I wish I were a different man, one who could offer you the life you want. The life you deserve. But it's just not in me."

Closing her eyes, Blair tried to memorize this moment. Without saying the words, Josh had just admitted he loved her. Just as she'd admitted the same to him. Blair had learned in the last few days that love was so much more than what you *did* for the other person; it was also what you *didn't* do. The choices you didn't force them to make.

Holding back her tears, Blair moved to his side of the table and gave him a soft kiss. Normally, their kisses were about caring, but not this time. The kiss they shared this time was about saying goodbye.

Chapter Ten

Josh stood by the door of the hospital room while Blair and her father, William Collins, visited with Eric. Josh felt like an interloper in this family scene—an unexpected and probably unwanted intruder. Her father had already made it clear he wasn't too enamored with Josh. The Harley had really ruffled the older man's feathers. And while William Collins spoke with his son and daughter, he kept shooting Josh suspicious glances. Josh felt like the big, bad wolf who'd been caught with Little Red Riding Hood.

He probably shouldn't have come to the hospital for this visit. But when Blair had asked him to come along, he hadn't had the heart to turn her down. Right now, there wasn't much he'd deny Blair.

Except the one thing she wanted . . . for him to stay permanently in Raynes.

William scoffed at something his son said, and Josh glanced at the older man. *Did Blair's father know how much he'd hurt his daughter all those years ago when he'd left her with her aunt?* You didn't need a thermometer to tell the man was cold. He held himself apart from his children. Big difference from the way Josh's dad was. His dad was a hugger. William Collins looked so stiff, he'd probably break if one of his kids hugged him.

But Josh would bet his boots that the man wanted to ask him about his relationship with Blair. Not that it mattered. His relationship with Blair, such as it had been, was over. They'd said their good-byes before her dad had even arrived.

Now all they had to do was make it through the next few hours. Then, after the performance and a short appearance at the cast party, he could head out of town. It didn't matter how far he made it tonight, just as long as he made it out of Raynes.

Almost against his will, Josh looked at Blair. He knew she was struggling to put on a happy face for her family, but he could see the sadness in her eyes, hear it in her voice.

"So, Blair, did you tell Dad how Josh saved that little girl?" Eric grinned at Josh. "Dad, I bet it's been a long time since you've met a real, live hero."

Muttering under his breath, Josh shot his friend a pointed look. *What was Eric doing?* He knew Josh hated this story, mostly because he hadn't been brave or a hero. He'd just done what anyone would have.

Still, after giving Josh an apologetic look, Blair explained what had happened. Probably out of consideration for him, she didn't embellish the details or drag out the story. She gave her father only the barest facts.

When she finished, Eric added, "But saving that little girl isn't the only thing that makes Josh brave. What makes him brave is that he hates heights. Can't stand them. Yet he faced his fear and did the right thing. In my book, that's a brave man. Don't you think so, Dad? It's not easy to face your fears. But Josh toughed it out."

Through narrowed eyes, Josh studied Eric. *What had prompted that outburst? The guy was acting weird. Eric had never done anything like this before.* Yet here he was, shoving Josh's weakness down his throat, almost as if he was trying to hack Josh off. Or make a not-so-subtle point.

Suddenly comprehension hit Josh: Eric knew. Somehow he'd figured out that his best friend had fallen for his sister. As far as Josh could tell, Eric was trying in his own backwards way to call him a coward for leaving. If Eric knew he loved Blair, it must show like a neon sign in the dead of night. Probably all of Raynes knew he loved her.

Blair's father nodded at Josh, then walked over and shook his hand. "Good job saving that child, Anderson. I know lots of men—" He shot a quick look at Blair. "And lots of women, too, who let their fear get the better of them."

Josh glanced at Blair, who looked as confused as he felt. She apparently hadn't figured out what her brother was up to yet.

"Dad, that's the kind of man Josh is," Eric continued. "He'll face his fear when it's the right thing to do. He'd never be a coward and run away."

Okay, now this was getting out of hand. Josh frowned at Eric. *Friend or not, what Eric was doing was wrong.*

Blair must have figured it out what was going on, because suddenly, she practically lunged out of the plastic chair she sat in.

"Let's go," she announced, smoothing her hands down the sides of her skirt and flashing a tight smile at her father. "Eric needs rest. Besides, we should grab something to eat before we go to the auditorium."

"Works for me," her father said with a shrug. Rather than embracing his injured son, he simply shook his hand. Then he followed Blair out the door. Josh waited until William was out of earshot, then he looked at Eric.

"There are a lot of things preventing me from

having a future with Blair," Josh said firmly. "It's not as simple as simply being brave."

"That's where you're wrong," Eric said. "You just haven't figured that out yet."

When they got back to the house, Josh announced he needed to run some errands before the performance. As Blair watched him drive away on his motorcycle, the sadness that had been growing inside her all day seemed to lodge in her heart. Which was silly, really. She knew he'd be back to do the play . . . he probably just wanted to get some air. Things were tense between them, and having her father watch them like bugs in a jar only made their last day together even more difficult.

With a sigh, Blair unlocked the front door, and her father followed her inside the house. After he was settled on the couch, she brought them both a glass of iced tea. She sat in the rocker facing him and braced herself for the impending conversation.

"So Josh Anderson is your idea of a Prince Charming," her father said with a bark of laughter.

Blair bristled but refrained from rising to his bait. She wasn't going to fight with her father. "Josh has done a terrific job in the play."

Her father gave her a narrowed-eyed look. "I wasn't talking about the play." Before she could respond, he added, "You've been crying."

"I haven't been crying, I'm just—"

Her father waved away her comment. "Eric's right. When I spoke to him on the phone a couple of days ago, he said you were in love with Josh."

Blair stilled. "Eric said that?"

Her father took a slow sip of his tea. "Yes. He also told me that Josh loves you, he just doesn't think he's right for you."

Blair knew all this. Hearing him reinforce her beliefs only weakened Blair's tentative hold on her emotions. "I know. He doesn't want to live here in Raynes. More importantly, his parents both have several failed marriages, and he thinks he doesn't have what it takes to make love last."

Her no-nonsense father made a snorting noise. "Then maybe you should be the one to change what you want in life. If you really love this man, then why in the world are you letting him go? Blair Marie Collins, I raised you to go after what you want in life, not to sit around boo-hooing when things don't go your way."

She didn't mean to be cruel, but before she could stop herself, Blair blurted out, "But you didn't really raise me at all. Mom did. Then Aunt Claire. You were rarely around."

Stunned at her own outburst, Blair covered her mouth with her trembling hand. She could see her words startled her father, but she didn't retract them.

She couldn't. For too many years, she'd kept her pain inside.

Eventually, her father nodded. "You're right. I didn't raise you. I didn't think I could do a good job. Claire was more qualified."

"No she wasn't. She didn't love me, or at least, not the way she should have. I was miserable being apart from you and Eric."

"We were all miserable after your mother died."

"But, Dad, I didn't just lose Mom. Only a few weeks after her death, I lost you and Eric, too. You left me at Aunt Claire's house." Blair felt tears stream down her face, and she impatiently brushed them away. For too many years she avoided discussing her painful past with her father, but no more. They needed to talk this out.

Suddenly, her father looked every one of his sixty-one years. "Guess I made a mistake. Maybe I wasn't brave enough to raise you. All I know is that after your mother died, I felt overwhelmed. I had no idea how to raise two kids."

"But you let Eric stay with you."

"Eric was almost sixteen. I knew what to do with a teenaged boy. But you were only twelve. I didn't know how to raise a girl."

A half-sob escaped Blair. "There's no right way, Dad. All I needed from you was your love and the security of my family."

"Then I'm sorry I took that from you." Silence fell on the room, the quiet tick of the grandfather's clock almost aggravating. To Blair, the noise only signaled how quickly her remaining hours with Josh were slipping away.

"I guess it doesn't matter anymore," Blair finally said.

"I don't know." William settled back on the couch. "I'm wondering if the past is why you're so fired up about staying in this town rather than going with Josh. Eric thinks you're looking for the love and security you lost years ago. I think I agree with him."

Blair resented being analyzed, especially by the man who had practically deserted her. But a kernel of truth lurked in his words. She did feel like she belonged in Raynes, like she was part of the community. It gave her immense satisfaction.

"I couldn't go with Josh, even if I wanted to," she said.

"Why not?"

That should be obvious. "Because I have a life here. I have my business. I have the play. My house. I can't walk away from my responsibilities."

Her father shook his head. "Those are just excuses. I've learned a lot in the years since your mother died. You don't get second chances. Ever. If you're sure Josh is the right one for you, you need to make room in your life for him. Tell me this, would you rather live in Raynes without this man or live in L.A. with him?"

The realization hit her that there was only one answer to that question. She'd moved to the small town so she could have a feeling of belonging. But being with Josh gave her that same feeling. She was going to be miserable living here without him. She no longer wanted to find a different man, someone who wanted to live in Raynes.

She wanted Josh.

Happiness flooded through Blair. "I'd rather live with Josh in a hut than live by myself in a palace," she said simply.

Her father nodded. "Good. Then make a list of everything you need to do so you can go, and tell him you'll meet him in Los Angeles in a few weeks."

Her father's no-nonsense attitude reminded her how many years he'd spent in the Army. To him, life was a simple matter of getting the job done, and in a way she had to admit he was right. Suddenly everything seemed so clear. Yes, she could do this. She *would* do this. "You're right. I need to offer to be with him, even if it means moving around a lot."

Her father chuckled. "See, that wasn't so hard, was it? And as for the failed marriages in his family, you tell Josh that you come from a long line of happy couples. I loved your mother deeply until the day she died. I still love her. So if he's worried you two can't make your love last, tell him he's wrong. Then set a date. I want to walk my daughter down the aisle before I die."

Blair smiled, her spirits soaring. "Yes, Dad. I promise."

Josh drove around aimlessly for an hour or so before he found himself at the interstate. Finally, tired and hungry, he pulled into a gas station parking lot and turned off the motorcycle's engine. Was Eric right? Was his leaving really hurting Blair rather than helping her? Sure, he knew she felt awful right now, but wouldn't she be better off in the long run? Wouldn't his leaving be like pulling a bandage off quickly? The pain was intense at first, but faded fast.

And Blair's pain *would* fade fast. He was certain of that. In a couple of weeks, she'd stop thinking about him. The rhythm of her life in Raynes would resume, and she'd stop missing him.

But he wouldn't stop missing her. He couldn't. She was in his heart, in his blood. Time and distance wouldn't change that . . . nothing would change that.

Sorry fool that he was, he'd end up missing Blair for the rest of his life.

Pulling his helmet off, Josh glanced around. Tourists bustled into the large convenience store, and eighteen-wheelers entered the parking lot for diesel fuel. Just a few miles out of Raynes, a whole different world existed. No one knew him here, no one congratulated him on saving Melanie or teased him about the play or scolded him for driving a motorcycle. Here, as in the rest of the world, he was invisible.

For the first time he could remember, he took no comfort in fading into the background. Being just a face in the crowd didn't feel safe anymore . . . it only felt lonely.

Josh hung his helmet on the handle of his motorcycle and scrubbed his face with weary hands. Images of Blair crowded his mind. Images of her smiling and laughing . . . and loving him. Always loving him. Pulling him into her world, into her heart. Easing the pain in his soul with her kisses and gentle touches.

Calm and clarity settled around him. Eric was right—it would take courage to stand and fight for the love he wanted. And there was always the chance he might fail. But even knowing the hazards, what sort of man was he if he didn't at least try? He had to be brave enough to face the past and brave enough to move on to the future.

Maybe Blair deserved someone better. But another man could never love her the way he did. No other man would cherish her the way he would.

Visions of smiling babies filled his mind. He knew deep in his heart he wanted that future with Blair. He wanted the family. He even wanted her gingerbread house he'd come to think of as home. Sure, there were no promises that every day would be wonderful, but life came with no guarantees. He couldn't always protect the important people in his life, he could only love them. He knew he had to treasure the time he had with Blair rather than throw away the best thing he'd ever had in his life.

Climbing off the motorcycle, Josh headed toward the pay phone. He needed to tell Ed Pattinola he couldn't take the job. It might be a great opportunity, but he wasn't leaving Raynes.

As he dialed, a new thought occurred to him. If Ed needed the help as badly as he claimed, he might be willing to arrange a remote contract. Josh could easily do a lot of the necessary work from an office set up in Blair's house.

He smiled. Hopefully, that house would soon be home to both of them.

Josh swung by Blair's house first, but he wasn't surprised to find he was too late. Since there was no answer at the door, he knew she'd probably headed over to the auditorium with her dad.

When he got to the auditorium, streams of ticket holders were waiting outside. Wanting to avoid other people, Josh came through the side door and spotted Blair immediately. Like a welcomed beam of moonlight on a dark night, she bustled around the actors and technicians, fixing problems, soothing nerves. Josh's spirit soared, and he headed across the stage.

Almost as if she sensed him, Blair looked up after he'd taken only a couple of steps. She stared at him for a few seconds. Then a slow smile formed on her sweet mouth. With a quick word to Leigh, Blair moved toward him.

"I was worried that you might have decided to leave early," she said softly when they reached each other.

"I thought about it," he admitted, drinking in the sight of her while he shored up his courage for the question he had to ask.

A little wariness lurked in her eyes. "So why did you come back?"

"For starters, I have to finish this play." Now that he was close to her, he could see a faint redness around the rim of her eyes. He felt terrible that he'd made her cry.

"Oh. Yes. The play." She sighed and glanced away from him.

"Yeah. The play. I made you a promise."

"I could have found someone to replace you." She looked directly at him, her hazel eyes weary. "But I'm glad you came back, even if it is only to finish the play." She drew in a deep breath, then said, "Josh, I think we should talk. About us."

"Yeah. Me, too." He took a step closer and laid a

hand on her arm, enjoying the little tingle that danced across his skin whenever he touched her.

Blair gazed at him with such love in her eyes that he felt his heart beat faster. "I've done a lot of thinking." She gave a short laugh. "That, and my dad told me what to do."

Confused, Josh tipped his head. "You've lost me."

"I thought I had. Lost you, I mean. But I realize now that if you want to live someplace else, that's fine with me. It may take me a little while to get everything settled here, but then I'd like to come to L.A. That is, if you want me to." She nibbled on her bottom lip. "I want to keep you in my life, Josh. I can't stand to lose you."

As she spoke, happiness filled up the emptiness deep inside Josh. She was willing to give up everything that mattered to her to be with him. He felt humbled by her love, and knew he'd spend the rest of his life making her dreams come true.

"Oh, Blair." He dipped his head and found her lips, kissing her deeply. When he finally lifted his head, he found himself grinning. "I don't want you to leave the life you have here."

Before he could continue, a sheen of tears appeared in her eyes. "Sorry. I guess I thought we might be able to work things out if I came to L.A."

She looked so miserable that Josh couldn't stand it.

"You don't understand. The reason you don't have to move to L.A. is that I'm staying here."

Blair blinked again. "Excuse me? What about your job?"

He chuckled and draped his arms around her waist. He knew the other cast members were watching them, but he didn't care. He didn't care if all of Raynes knew what was happening—the whole world was welcome to know he loved Blair Collins.

"You know, your brother is a pretty smart guy. With all his comments about bravery this afternoon, he finally got it through my thick skull that I have to face some old fears if I want to have a future with you. And I *do* want that future. I love you too much to leave. So I spoke to the contract manager in L.A. and told him I couldn't take the job . . . unless he agreed to let me work from here. He wasn't happy about it, but he said yes. I'll have to fly to L.A. every six weeks or so for meetings, but the rest of the time I can work from Raynes."

He leaned his forehead against hers, breathing in her soft perfume. "Now if I can only find a place to stay while I'm in town. You know, Raynes doesn't have a hotel."

Blair's laugh came out as a half-sob. Tears ran down her cheeks. "You're kidding, right?"

"No, ma'am. I'm very serious."

She stood in front of him, crying and smiling at the same time. "You're really willing to live in Raynes?"

He pulled her close in a tight hug. "Yes. I am. But I have to warn you, I'm an old-fashioned guy. I'm afraid I have to insist we get married."

This time, Blair laughed and twined her arms around his neck. "I love you. I love you," she said.

"That's good. Because I love you, too."

"Really?"

Josh grinned, loving Blair, loving the life he knew he would have with her. "Oh, yeah. Really. And I thought we might want to start a family soon. Raynes strikes me as a great place to raise kids. I figure I'll probably be pretty good at coaching soccer."

This time, when Blair started crying, he knew her tears were those of happiness. He felt the same joy running through his veins.

"You haven't told me whether you'll marry me or not," he pointed out.

"Yes." Blair said the single word firmly, then added, "Yes, yes, yes."

Leaning up, she kissed him, and they were still kissing when Theresa walked over.

"Yeow," she said loudly, and Josh reluctantly released Blair's lips. "That's one great kiss, but if Josh doesn't change into his costume soon, we aren't going to have a Prince Charming in the play tonight."

Josh smiled at Blair, love filling his heart. "I'll go

get dressed," he told her. But before he walked away, he leaned down to Blair and whispered in her ear, "Just so you know, after tonight, I'm only playing Prince Charming for you."

Blair laughed, happiness radiating from her. "It's a deal."

Then, in front of most of the population of Raynes, Texas, Josh once more kissed the woman who'd come to mean more than anything to him. Together, he knew, they'd find a way to make their love last forever.